Second
Time
Around

Second Time Around

Christina Bartolomeo

PIATKUS

First published in Great Britain in 1998 by
Judy Piatkus (Publishers) Ltd of
5 Windmill Street, London W1

This edition published 1998

A catalogue record for this book is available from the British Library.

ISBN 0 7499 3040 3 (pbk)

Set in 11/13 pt Times by
Phoenix Photosetting, Chatham, Kent

Printed and bound in Great Britain by
Mackays of Chatham PLC, Chatham, Kent

Chapter I

My sister Francesca's phone calls are always like a summons – even the ring has an imperious quality.

'You have to be there,' she said. I knew exactly how her mouth would look as she said this, like a nun's mouth, all pruney and prissy. The mouth of a woman who still keeps a stack of gilt-edged holy cards, earned by grade school good behavior, in the back of her bureau drawer.

'I can make up an excuse.'

'His last birthday you said you had chicken pox. You had chicken pox twice as a kid.'

'Like he's going to remember.'

'He's seventy-one. How many more years do you think we're going to have him?'

How many, I wonder. How damn many. People like my father were capable of living to ninety-six out of sheer spite.

It was a Monday morning in late July, and I was standing in my shop, going through a new consignment. While Francesca went on about the details, I inspected a 1941 French-blue twill jacket with sixteen covered buttons down the front. I wanted it for myself, but suspected it would look better on my sister Cynthia. Cynthia was as different from Francesca as I was from both of them, and the thought of what she would say about Francesca's scheme cheered me as I listened to Francesca debate menu, guest list, and whether or not to set

up a tent in the back yard. I am woefully undomestic, while
Francesca can spend twenty minutes comparing the merits of
competing brands of vacuum cleaner bags.

This party was not a family tradition, but part of the clumsy
process of consoling my father for my mother's death two
summers ago. Before, we'd never made much fuss over my
father's birthday. He was the sort of man who discouraged
fuss. And after all, everyone on his side of the family lived to
a ripe old age, driving their nearest and dearest crazy and
finally dying peacefully in their sleep.

You wouldn't have thought my father needed much consoling. Our parents' marriage had not been a happy one.
My generation may be marked by the common observation
that all our parents loved each other *once* – a brief shining
moment over long before our memories started, like the
Kennedy administration. But no one can ever understand
what holds a marriage together, what fear of the chaos of
separation, what deep unadmitted need. And of course, for
American Catholics who married in the 1950s, divorce was
a tragedy. It was an end to your standing in the Church, a
disgrace to your family. In the parish where I grew up
wife-beating and child abuse were not unknown, nor was
the sort of 'benign' repressed homosexuality of the gym-
teacher and choir-director variety. But it was the few
divorces that elicited the *most* shocked whispers. And my
mother and father felt it as a personal betrayal when Jackie
Kennedy married a divorced man.

My parents had shared some variety of affection, but it was
so far from what I wanted or hoped for that I didn't dare to
contemplate it. Simply said, my mother's death had been an
awful shock to my father's system. Ever since, he had been
dwelling on his own inevitable demise. He would sigh an
exaggerated Southern Italian sigh, and hope we'd pray for
him after he was gone. He'd wonder out loud if he'd be per-

mitted into Heaven, given that three of his children, myself included, had fallen away from the Church.

He visited my mother's grave every Sunday afternoon to complain about us. No effort at sympathy or affection got through – in fact, he gave the impression that he'd been saddled with us by my mother, although all his children were independent and he rattled around his big square brick house in the Maryland suburbs like a pea in a tin can. My brothers Dom and Joey and my sister Annette paid weekly visits of homage. Francesca stopped by every few days in her role of Devoted Catholic Daughter. I went only when cajoled by my brothers or bullied by my older sister.

A party, Francesca had decided in her numbskulled way, was just the thing to cheer my father up. I knew how she'd go about this. She'd get on the phone to all his paysanne buddies, his old clients (my father was a retired, never-very-successful real estate agent), and several widows with whom he played cards. She'd bully him into purchasing a new shirt. She'd cook four huge pans of manicotti. And she'd extract a hundred-dollar contribution from each of us for this extravaganza. It was a contribution I could ill afford, since my business, a used clothing shop called The Second Time Around, was on its last legs.

Pleasing my father was easy for Francesca. She was married to a pillar of her parish and had three strapping boys my father adored. I was my father's least favorite daughter, and he was a man who should have had only sons. I was like my mother's side of the family: pale, quiet, slow to anger. My father was a fine father for his robust, contentious children, and uncomfortable in the same room with me.

'Just what I need, Francesca, a family occasion to dread.'

'How can you talk that way about your own relatives?' said Francesca.

Because they exhaust me, I wanted to tell her. Because

after a few hours this Campanella family gathering would feel
like a siege in its tenth month. I didn't say this to my sister, of
course. She had never encouraged the exchange of sisterly
confidences. All I knew about her was what she showed the
world: a good Catholic wife and mother, who worked in a
doctor's office four days a week.

'I'll bring a salad,' I said, 'but I'm *not* coming early.'

'Did I ask you? You're useless in the kitchen anyway.'

I'm all right in other rooms of the house, I thought but
didn't say. In our whole lives Francesca and I had never once
talked about sex.

Now she said, 'Dad told you to buy him something practical for a change.'

'Nothing I get him makes him happy. I could show up with
a piece of the True Cross and he'd fuss about it.'

She sighed, the annoyed little sigh she'd been emitting
around me ever since I could remember.

'Just be there, okay? Bring what's his name. I'll call you
with more details.'

She rang off, and I stood for a moment trying to regain my
equilibrium. The place was empty, as it was nearly every
weekday morning. I'd brought The Second Time Around
nearly a year before, and wasn't making much of a go of it.
Faithful old customers and lovers of vintage clothes still wandered in, regulars from the woman who had owned the shop
before me, but you couldn't build a business on those few
stalwarts.

Summer had come to complete the slump. The heat drained
people of the desire to do anything but get out of town. Today
was the sort of glaring summer day that reminded you that the
city of Washington was built on a swamp and used to be considered a hardship assignment by foreign diplomats. The sun
came white through the windows and a siren whined in the
distance. Another hot one, the announcer on the classical

music station said, then fell silent in favor of three Chopin preludes.

When the last note had faded into the still air, I called Philip, who was, technically speaking, my fiance. In other words, the matter had been mentioned, but there has never been a slower amble to the altar.

'Francesca's organizing this big party,' I said. 'My father's birthday.'

'That's nice of her.'

'No it's not. It's just another club to beat me with. Francesca lives for that.'

'She cares about your dad, that's all.'

At least *she* cares, I could hear him finish silently. Philip has always been shocked over my dearth of appropriate family feeling. I could picture him at his desk at Anthony, Truitt, Marlow and Strouse, wearing one of his excellent suits (light gray gabardine), making his steady way through a stack of papers, examining them through the tortoise-shell glasses that made him look like Clark Kent.

Philip was good at his job. His clients thought of him as priest, psychiatrist and white knight rolled into one. They called him at all hours. They valued his opinion. They felt that if Philip believed in their essential innocence, the forces of outraged justice (usually in the shape of the IRS) would understand too.

'Remind me of the date,' said Philip. He was hoping against hope he'd have an ironclad engagement. Philip seemed unnerved by my family and treated them with a gingerly politeness which they made fun of behind his back.

'You're not getting out of this,' I said.

'Just tell me the date.'

'August twenty-fifth.'

'Will Cynthia be there?'

'Of course.'

My sister Cynthia and Philip didn't get along. He disapproved of her career choices.

Cynthia had left home for New York at seventeen to become a serious stage actress. Three years of waitressing and roles in student films, off-off-off Broadway plays and B movies followed. In one movie she played a space alien. In another, called *Love Crazy*, she was knifed in a shower before the opening credits.

It was in *Love Crazy* that she caught the eye of a photographer for *Purrr* magazine. Six months later she was voted Kitten of the Year. She was one of the most popular centerfolds in the history of the magazine. She guested on radio programs where the prize for the lucky caller was a date with her. She flew around the country attending auto shows and charity softball games. The magazine put her on retainer and supplied her with a closetful of flashy evening gowns. Every time she spent a day signing autographs or had her picture taken with storm window magnates at the storm window company convention, they paid her an extra one hundred fifty dollars.

She'd said goodbye to all that when she got a lucrative contract as the *RosePetal*'s catalog girl. *RosePetal*'s was one of the most successful purveyors of 'sensuous lingerie' in the country, and Cynthia was their star model. 'An icon of sexuality' one young men's magazine had called her. Philip hated her notoriety. Or was it her fame?

For her part, Cynthia could never forgive Philip for having been born with a silver spoon in his mouth. He was the son of Hood Traynor, the former senator from Montville, Alabama, fourth of the Traynors to serve in Congress. Philip had gone to a private boarding school, then on to Harvard and Harvard Law. He had stepped into his current lucrative job rather than applied for it. He worked hard. But he'd never had to work just to win the chance to prove himself, which made all the difference between his class and ours, ours being what you could call the scrappy lower middle class. Cynthia felt Philip didn't acknowledge his advantages, and treated him with a brisk contempt.

'I just wish we could skip this,' I said to Philip.

'It's your family. Of course we have to be there.'

A minute later, his other line buzzed.

'I have to go, okay? Something light for dinner tonight if you don't mind. It's so hot.'

The new consignment had filled four grocery bags which had been dumped on my counter by a frazzled middle-aged woman disposing of her late mother's things. I explained the policy: a sixty-forty split, with prices reduced twenty percent every month that the garments didn't sell. She looked dubious.

'But these will sell,' I reassured her. 'These forties jackets are very hot right now.' So hot, I thought to myself, that it doesn't matter that you didn't have them dry-cleaned the way I usually ask for them. They smelled of cedar and some faint perfume probably not even bottled anymore.

'If you say so,' she said.

'Your mother had wonderful taste, Mrs. Piewtrotski.'

'They've been lying around the attic. I couldn't persuade her to get rid of them.'

Get rid of them! After she left, I wondered how her mother, a woman who so obviously loved clothes, could have had a daughter like that, someone who would actually leave the house in a bright pink polo shirt and madras plaid shorts that pulled at the hips. Someone who at forty tied her greying hair back in an enormous grosgrain bow, with that sickly girlishness that afflicts women's dress in this town. But then it was often that way, glamorous mothers with dowdy offspring. A lot of my consignments arrived on the wings of daughterly resentment.

I didn't deal in vintage couture stuff, to my deep sorrow. People were too aware of what's valuable nowadays, collectors too avid. But I got good modern secondhand designer stuff, Calvin Klein, Donna Karan, Ralph Lauren, Valentino. And vintage American fashion, the kind with yellowed ILGWU labels inside and tags that said, 'Roxbury's of Detroit' or whatever upper-middle-class department store originally sold the line back in 1948. It was a weird mix, the modern designer clothes and the vintage garments, hanging side by side. So weird that perhaps it put people off.

Besides the French blue jacket, there was a brown-and-black miniature plaid with a black velvet collar, a bias-cut peach satin nightgown and an evening blouse of black net, pintucked down the front, with a flat silk collar. Hardy yet delicate old beauties, made back when hems didn't fall out and buttons stayed put.

Looking at the pale silk stockings saved in their original flat cardboard boxes, I thought the dear departed must have been like me, marking each milestone in her life by what she was wearing. If I were ever drowning, my life would flash before my eyes as a series of darling outfits, from my dotted-swiss First Communion dress to the hideous mint-green Quiana floral I wore to my junior prom. Not only can I chronicle my own history this way, I can remember what my sisters were wearing on all their big occasions, too. For example, I could still embarrass Francesca by mentioning the lilac sateen empire-waisted gown she'd chosen for the St. John's Military Academy Winter 1975 Regimental Ball.

I got this talent from my mother, who was raised in a tenement in Boston. When she was a child and my carpenter grandfather was out of work, my mother had been dressed in castoffs from the Salvation Army Barrel or the Baptist church donation pile. At fourteen, she'd sit on the Boston Common and instead of looking at boys, dream of owning the fancy dresses she saw on rich women walking by. When she was nineteen, she got herself a job at the Raytheon factory and saved up enough money for charm school courses at John Powers, where they taught her how to dress and how to walk. On the advice of a teacher there, she freed her voice of its slum-cockney accent by listening to tapes of Shakespeare, Tennyson and Longfellow. When I was a child, she would recite 'Evangeline' to us at bedtime. I can still hear her intoning: '*This* is the *forest* prim*eval*.'

She came to Washington in the late fifties, as a Grade Three secretary at the Pentagon. When she stepped off the train, she owned only three outfits: a black dress, princess-seamed with a white Peter Pan collar; a turquoise silk coat with a matching sheath in charcoal shantung silk with turquoise accents, and a full-skirted, tight-bodiced wool challis printed all over with autumn leaves. I had often heard her describe these clothes, in the fond tones of one remembering friends who have passed on. She also owned two bras and a girdle, specially fitted at the best lingerie shop in Boston, and three pairs of lace-trimmed silk underwear, which she washed out in the sink at the Dolly Madison Hotel for Women every night. She would eat at Sholl's Cafeteria for a week to pay for a new pair of stockings.

All her life, my mother saved for months for one new dress. While other mothers were content with polyester pantsuits from Sears, my mother insisted on things with pedigree. Who could blame her for clinging to Chanel No. 5 and restrained little suits from Lord and Taylor's when her own mother had worn a cheap perfume called Evening in Paris and baggy flowered housedresses with grimy string belts?

The phone rang again.

'Is it too damn hot or what?' said a trained, throaty voice. On the phone, Cynthia sounded like some ballsy forties screen heroine. In person, this image of feminist assurance was dimmed by her blinding sex appeal.

'Cynthia! What's up?' She rarely called me in the middle of the morning, usually waiting until midnight or three a.m. – whenever the urge took her.

'Nothing. Everything. Did Francesca call you yet?'

'Yeah.'

'Well, I'm pissed, Diana.'

'About the party?'

'No. It's Simon. He has no time for me these days. No time at all.'

'Well, Olivia did just come back, Cynthia.'

'We all knew she was coming back. I mean, her body was lost in a swamp, for God's sake. I don't know how a mortician stays in business in that town.'

'The point is, Simon's like all men. They think work is where they have to prove themselves and they can coast on credit with you.'

Simon, Cynthia's lover, played Brice Covington on *Covington Heights*, the second most popular soap opera in the country. I watched *Covington Heights*. All my friends watched *Covington Heights*. Executives installed tiny televisions in their offices on which to watch *Covington Heights* and secretaries gathered in conference rooms to watch breathless. Recently, the Post Style Section had done an article about college kids who skipped class to watch *Covington Heights*.

Brice Covington was the oldest Covington son, a tortured, Byronic soul. For ten years, Simon had portrayed Brice's struggle to free himself from the stifling burden of his family's wealth and position. To do this, he had become a reporter, then a seminarian, and then an agent for a benevo-

lent worldwide spy organization. Brice had been on the scene
of more international catastrophes than NATO.

Brice's wife Olivia had returned from the dead a week
before. Now his faithful audience was wondering when he'd
notice his resurrected spouse wasn't really the beloved Olivia,
who had been his childhood sweetheart and who had suppos-
edly died in an explosion during a Latin American revolution.
It was her evil twin Charmaine. Brice, whom plot reasons frequently required to be criminally stupid, hadn't caught on yet.

We never saw Simon down in D.C. He had a grueling
schedule, especially when his storyline was on the front
burner. I'd met him once in New York, though. In person, he
was paler and less forceful than on the show, but still invested
with a powerful, sad charm. Over the years as Brice, he had
acquired a slight British accent. (Brice had gone to prep
school in England, for which he had departed at the age of ten
and from which he returned at nineteen, only two years later).
In real life, Simon hailed from Toledo.

'It's not just the show. I can take the schedule, the hours, all
that. It's Delia,' said Cynthia.

Delia was Simon's real-life wife. Cynthia had met Simon
two years ago on the set of a margarine commercial, the day
after Delia moved out. Simon and Cynthia were similar in that
way to the characters on *Covington Heights* – while most of
our lives have breathing spaces, lulls, and finger-twiddling
time, events follow thick and fast for these children of fate.

'Delia's dragging her heels on the settlement. One minute
she wants to break his kneecaps, the next minute she wants to
have his baby. And he's putting up with it! He's putting up
with all her antics "because she needs me more than you do,
Cynthia." We had a huge fight last night.'

'He should watch it. Doesn't he realize that you could have
anybody you want?'

This was the simple truth.

'I don't want anybody. I want Simon. But let's not talk about it. I'll get upset, and I have a callback in an hour. Anyway, how's the business?'

Cynthia was the only person in my family who took an interest in my shop. The rest of them were mortified that I'd quit a perfectly good job as a policy analyst in the Department of Nuclear Energy's Nonmilitary Radioactive Waste Storage Division in order to sell what Francesca called, 'other people's nasty old clothes'.

'The shop's lousy.'

'When I come down for Dad's big wingding you can show me the new stuff.'

Cynthia was one of my best customers. Of course I gave her everything at cost. She looked especially beautiful in vintage clothes. They brought out the integrity of her bone structure, the heartbreaking shape of her mouth. But then, Cynthia looked beautiful in everything, even the leather bustiers and silk polyester negligees she wore as the *RosePetal*'s model.

As the *RosePetal*'s girl, Cynthia had appeared all over town in bus stop ads the previous Christmas, wearing a red velvet bodysuit and a little Santa cap. This past spring she'd been on subway billboards in a bra and panties constructed entirely of silk violets, with the tagline, 'Give her flowers that won't wilt.' She had her own infomercial. There was even talk of a calendar.

At least the *RosePetal*'s stuff was tame enough for my father to know about. No one had told him about the spread in *Purrr*, and since the only periodical he subscribed to was the Catholic Standard, he wasn't likely to find out. The *Purrr* business was pretty mild – Cynthia strictly by herself, in a variety of time-honored poses. But my father wouldn't have seen it that way. So the family kept quiet. It was part of our tradition of not telling my father things that would make the vein in his forehead throb.

'Although after all,' my mother had said when Cynthia did the first spread, 'it isn't so different from being an artist's model.'

'Artist's models don't usually have their tongues between their teeth and their hands between their legs,' I said.

'It's very tasteful, considering,' said my mother, who had always been awed and delighted by Cynthia's glamor.

Cynthia began describing to me a fight she had had with a salesgirl at Bendel's.

'I said, this is not an irregularity in the fabric, this is a grease spot. I know a grease spot when I see it. And she says in this snooty voice, how do I know you didn't get that on there yourself? So I told her to let me see her manager. And then when the manager came she said, well madam, you should have checked this item before you purchased it. And I said, don't you call me madam in that snotty tone of voice. Let me see *your* manager if you can't give me satisfaction. By the time I left they were all crying.'

Life for Cynthia was a constant battle, between living in New York and holding her own in a business that broke gentler spirits and more delicate talents than hers. Luckily, she brought unbeatable stamina to the fight. Her voice on the phone was as reviving as a glass of cold lemonade. Being related to her made me feel like a more interesting person, just as being related to Francesca made me feel exhausted and colorless.

'So about Delia,' I said. 'Why don't you put your foot down?'

'He's in such a panic right now I can't risk it. He's overwhelmed with guilt at ending his marriage.'

'He's done it enough on TV.'

'TV is different. He's not the same as Brice Covington, even though people always mix them up. Remember when I was seeing Dracula?'

She had had a brief affair with a man playing Dracula on Broadway. She had been attracted by his toothy masterfulness until she realized he was nothing at all like the character he played with such sinister perfection. In fact, he organized his sock drawer by color and worried about dietary fiber. He also had what Cynthia referred to as 'a mushy behind'. Physical perfection in men was important to Cynthia. She was beautiful. It was understandable that she would want a beautiful man. The trouble with most of the beautiful men she had fallen for was that by the time they reached adulthood and learned how much their beauty would let them get away with, they were of no use to any woman who wanted more than the honor of being seen with them. For real value, give me a guy whose face has character and who had to wear glasses at an early age; that's the sort of thing that instils sweetness and empathy.

We talked awhile. She asked me to save the French blue jacket for her. Then she said, 'Diana, do you ever miss Mom?'

'Yeah. But then I missed her when she was alive, too.'

'I know what you mean. We took care of her more than she ever took care of us. Still, I miss her so much. She was only fifty-eight. Talk about being cheated.'

'You can go crazy trying to figure that part out.'

'She used to get such a kick out of birthday presents. Not like Dad. Well, anyway, you buy whatever you want to for him. Buy him an enema bag, that's what he deserves, the way he treats you. I'd better go. I want to call Michael about redoing my head shots. I told him to go for a vampy effect and he made me look hard.'

While I ate my lunch, tuna on a bagel, I thought about my mother. She had always been frail – the family euphemism for 'alcoholic'. We'd spent most of our childhood caring for her, watching to see that she didn't fall downstairs when she was drinking, bringing her tea and toast during hangovers, making her excuses when she failed to show up for school plays and mother-daughter lunches.

My mother's death was not simple and swift. One May night my father had found her unconscious on the bathroom floor. At first he thought it was just the usual thing. When he couldn't wake her up, efficient men arrived in an ambulance and sped off with her to Georgetown Hospital. It turned out she had a bleeding blood vessel at the base of her skull. They patched that one up, then found another one, and another. All that June and July the doctors discovered time bombs in her head. Three 'successful' operations which were later written up in an article for the *New England Journal of Medicine*, and finally a heart attack – her exhausted body's way of avoiding further well-meant torture.

But in between, there were many weeks in the hospital. I'd visit her every day. She always asked for the latest fashion magazines. I bought *Vogue* and *Bazaar* and *Woman's Wear Daily*, then I started getting the foreign fashion magazines from the international newspaper shop on Dupont Circle – British and French and Italian *Vogue*. French *Elle* and British *Elle*. We would go over them page by page, my mother approving or disapproving, examining every detail. After the magazines were consumed, we watched soap operas. She liked to criticize the way the actresses looked. She particularly admired Erica on 'All My Children' because Erica was short like my mother, dressed so well, and had such good posture. 'That Erica,' my mother would say, 'she's got them all fooled'.

One afternoon I brought her the Australian *Vogue*. I was wearing a khaki-green trench coat, I remember, because it was a summer of sudden storms. After the second operation, my mother had had a stroke that played hell with her speech, but I still knew exactly what she thought of the Pre-Raphaelite look favored in the fall runway shows. She thought it was sloppy and ridiculous, while I liked the emphasis on wild hair and pale, pale skin, since my own skin is very pale and my dark hair is curly and unmanageable.

We had a wonderful afternoon. The nurse brought us two Jello parfaits on the lunch tray. The soaps were full of incident. When Cynthia came to replace me and I was about to leave, my mother tugged my arm urgently. I leaned down. She whispered, 'Green not good on you,' in her stroke-garbled voice. Those were the last words she ever spoke to me – a final motherly gesture.

At the Gallucci Brothers funeral home ('Tasteful funerals for Catholic families since 1932'), Cynthia and Francesca quarreled about what my mother's body should wear, even though the coffin was closed. People who have had brain surgery don't make the prettiest corpses. Francesca wanted the brown crepe shirtwaist that my mother kept for funerals. Cynthia favored the ruby-red number my mother had worn for our sister Annette's wedding. It draped scandalously low in the back. No mother-of-the-bride dress for Grace Bellafiore!

Francesca left orders for the brown dress. But Cynthia sneaked back to the home and countermanded Francesca's instructions. Francesca didn't find out until the night after the funeral. What a commotion that was, Francesca and Cynthia putting away the leftovers and screaming at each other.

They buried my mother in Fort Lincoln cemetery out in Prince George's County, in a new section at the edge of a field. It had the barren look of subdivisions under construction. Sometimes I worry about her alone out there, with all those newly bought, untenanted graves around her. Sometimes I think about our last afternoon at the hospital, how in the shadow of death my mother had been happy reading her fashion magazines, as if she were about to spring up from bed and go shopping. I try not to think of these things. I hope Heaven is a cocktail party full of incident and that my mother is there in her red dress, the center of attention just as she loved to be, holding a perfect martini in her hand.

Chapter II

My shop was on the second floor of a dingy side street off Wisconsin Avenue, three blocks from the cathedral. My apartment was on Connecticut Avenue, which ran parallel to Wisconsin half a mile away. I glanced up at the window as I left. Some of the gold-peel lettering was flaking off, giving the name a flyblown air. The white summer light showed up the smears and streaks made by pigeon droppings on the glass. The place looked already defunct.

I walked home down the leafy hill of Newark Street. The houses in this neighborhood had been the summer homes of Victorian families. Cleveland Park started that way, separate from the city, so separate still that when you stood at the top of this hill you could hear only the wind in the old oaks and maples. The houses were frosted and festooned like wedding cakes and were painted the colors of sugar roses – eggshell, pale pink and cerulean blue. They had generous porches like the wide lap of a favorite aunt, and in the gardens through the year you could find marigolds, hyacinths, roses and lilac. Now, in high summer, only the roses remained, drooping on their stems.

I had nothing in the house to eat and only an hour before Philip arrived. So I took the shortcut halfway down the hill, through a cobblestoned alley where milk and ice were once delivered. My Italian grandfather, who had been a knife-sharpener in a rattling green truck, used to come round to knock at these doors.

At the market I bought some chicken breasts to broil, wild rice, and romaine and cucumbers for a salad. It was just as uninventive as the first dinner we'd had together, during a fundraiser for Virginia Democrats at the Alexandria Holiday Inn one November night.

I'd been raised on the Maryland side of the river and lived in the city since I'd been twenty-one, so I was innocent as a baby about Virginia politics. But my boss at the time wanted our office to make a good showing. That was how I found myself eating too-pink roast beef and talking to Philip, who'd come in late and been forced to sit at the insignificant table.

'You're braver than I am,' was the first thing he said to me. 'You're managing to eat this stuff.'

'I'm hungry. I didn't realize they'd keep us standing around for an hour without so much as a peanut.'

'That's the rule at these things. You need a free hand to glad-hand.'

'Are you a lobbyist?' I asked him.

'Nope. I'm a lawyer. Another kind of lowlife.'

He didn't look like a lowlife, but then Washington is home to many impeccably dressed reptiles. He wore a dark blue suit and a tie with a print like William Morris wallpaper. His eyes were a pure blue-green, a blue-green so clear that they would have been startling, except that they were half-concealed by heavy golden-brown eyelashes that gave him a shy and sleepy look.

We talked through the bloody roast beef, the gelid chocolate mousse, the tongue-pickling coffee, the pastel after-dinner mints. I liked listening to his low voice with its Alabama accent, admiring his lovely eyes and French cuffs. He looked at you when he talked, really looked at you. I was used to Hill types whose eyes would roam over your head, flicking back

and forth in search of more important prey. He didn't tell me
he was a former senator's son until the dessert came, and even
then he said it sheepishly, like an embarrassing secret that he
may as well get out in the open early.

When he asked me if I'd have dinner with him sometime, I
said yes, dazzled and intimidated. We spent a series of polite
and quiet evenings: a small French restaurant, a chamber
music concert, a revival of *Lawrence of Arabia* at the Uptown
theater. At the end of each of these civilized little dates, he
walked me courteously to the front door and said a chaste
goodnight.

Time passed and he didn't make his move. Was he gay?
Was he engaged to some girl back home? Even worse – was
he straight and unattracted to me? Finally I asked him to dinner at my apartment, where I served him a ten-dollar steak
with baked potatoes and steamed asparagus. Most men
respond well to meals where great hunks of meat play the star
role.

After dinner, we sat on the couch, drinking our brandy. He
told me about an Irish setter he'd had as a boy. Outside the
wind howled. It was one of those bitterly cold winter nights
when no one wants to be alone.

I interrupted the dog story.

'Philip. You're not gay, are you?'

He laughed.

'No, I'm not gay. What gave you the idea I was gay?'

'Well, for one thing, you're sitting way over at that end of
the sofa.'

'Maybe I'm just waiting for an invitation to sit closer.'

'Sit closer,' I said.

He sat closer. He began to play with my fingers. He stroked
my wrist with his thumb.

'So what do you think?' he said after a minute.

'What do I think about what?'

'Now that you've gotten to know me.'

'I think you're a nice guy.'

'Ouch.'

'I mean I like you. I really do.'

'You like me, huh?'

He started to kiss my neck, under my left earlobe.

'Do you like me, Philip?'

'I kept asking you out, if you noticed.'

We didn't talk much after that. We were busy with other things. It's the quiet types you have to watch out for.

The next morning, he got up and made pancakes while I ran out for the paper. We sat at my tiny wrought-iron kitchen table reading and eating our pancakes. I liked mine drenched in syrup with lots of bacon and a glass of cold milk to finish them off. Philip liked only a dab of syrup, no butter, and limited his bacon to two slices. When he'd finished the editorial page, he drank some coffee and fiddled with his cup and saucer until I looked over at him. Then he said, 'Would it be all right with you if I'm around for a while?'

'You mean the rest of the day?'

'No, I mean a regular thing. I could become quite attached to you.'

His heavy lashes were down over his eyes. I couldn't see his expression, so I went over and sat in his lap. I put my arms around him.

'It's all right by me,' I said.

That had been three years ago. We'd passed our thirtieth birthdays. Since then I'd been thinking about the rest of my life and looking around me, and I didn't like what I saw.

I have been witness to all kinds of love. Happy love at first sight that went on to sweet domesticity. Wild, eventful affairs (I'd specialized in these before I met Philip). Divorces in which the two partners were like vultures tearing apart a carcass. And, of course, I had several single friends who had simply given up, exhausted by the search, whose deepest relationships were now with a cat or dog.

In all this observation of love in its varieties, I hadn't learned a damn thing. I hadn't drawn forth any useful generalities or found any rules to live by.

For any hints about connubial bliss my parents could offer, we might as well have been raised by wolves. My mother and father lived in a time when American Catholics followed the party line and used the rhythm method. Using the rhythm method, they acquired six children, when actually they had barely enough love between them for each other. At some point before I was born, my mother began to drink. Sometime later, my father – my father who looked so handsome in his photos from the War, my father who had broken so many hearts when he married my mother – got fat. My mother drank and confided her sorrows to us. My father stewed and raged, sometimes at her and sometimes at his children.

The marriage was like some horrible play. There were only two characters, but they never addressed each other directly. They did all their speaking in asides to the audience.

My mother would watch my father suck the marrow out of a chicken bone with an expression on her face that said, How did this brute wander in here? My father would return from a rough day at work to find my mother sleeping it off, and his face would droop like a sad old bulldog's. Sometimes they would go out together – to a wedding or funeral or office party, and for the instant before they left they would look young and spruce and happy. But they'd always come home fighting.

So marriage was something grownups did and later regretted, and it was no accident that the men I fell for during my twenties were always on their way to somewhere else. Hugh joined the Foreign Service and left for Turkey. John worked for a senator from Oklahoma who lost his reelection bid. Sidney was teaching a guest semester in political science at Georgetown. My love life was like standing perpetually on the edge of a dock, waving men goodbye.

Then I met Philip. Philip wasn't going anywhere. His life was in Washington and had always been. Philip's family was one of those Southern political families who really own this town. They are like courtiers or civil servants, outlasting presidents and pundits and the whims of faithless voters.

Philip's grandfather had been mayor of Montville for thirty years. Some Traynor second cousin had helped author the Missouri Compromise. A distant in-law had signed the Declaration of Independence. In the tapestry of American history, the Traynors were a continuous indigo thread. To me, this permanency seemed a wonderful, frightening luxury. On Philip's part, I think I was a welcome relief from the legislative assistants, rising young lawyers, and hometown belles he'd been used to. With them, he was part of a careful game plan, an appropriate partner with the right credentials.

When everything about a person's life charms you – his background, his possessions, his flawless manners and meticulously generous lovemaking – it is hard to discern whether you are charmed by *him*. I never stopped to ask myself what life would be like if Philip and I were stranded on a desert island, away from his gracious background and my endless capacity to be impressed by his polish and poise. Even the little things delighted me. It delighted me that Philip's socks were always the right length, never showing that pale shankskin that middleclass bureaucrats too often reveal. It delighted me that he never inspected a bill in a restaurant in that anxious way of people who have to be careful about money. It delighted me to follow his drawly Alabama accent as you'd follow the words to an obscure ballad. It delighted me that Philip's life had been like an ocean cruise with all the amenities provided, while mine had been a hot noisy subway ride. I wanted to be on that cruise with Philip. I wanted to escape with him into the cerulean heights from which he and his kind viewed the world. That place looked so cool, blue and restful.

On the other hand ... on the other hand, we never ate Chinese food in bed, like Woody Allen and Mariel Hemingway did in that great scene from *Manhattan*. We never called in sick and stayed home to fool around or catch the afternoon matinee at the Uptown – his work was too weighty, too pressing. We never took ballroom dancing classes at the Vic Daumit School right in the neighborhood, although I had always wanted to and mentioned it from time to time.

I'd learned to think of these little yearnings of mine as silly, as having nothing to do with the questions of real love, which were about whether two people could coexist amiably and manage not to bore each other too much of the time. We could certainly do that. We rarely fought, never had those hot sticky quarrels some of our friends suffered through as they wrangled their way to matrimony or separation. (I didn't long for these after watching my parents' fights, in which anything became fair game and a scorched earth policy prevailed.) Philip and I both had the sort of superficial intelligence that had allowed Philp to ace the law boards and me to score in the 90th percentile on my SATs, so we could discuss anything from the situation in Chechnya to the return of the double-breasted suit for fall. And if the heartwrenching or sidesplitting subjects I sometimes wanted to bring up were somehow always squelched by Philip's lack of interest – well, when you move from hanging off a subway pole to sipping sherry in a stateroom on the Queen Mary, you should expect a more confining decorum. It's the price of admission.

Our life together was so serene, its tenor so even, that I shut
my eyes and breathed a sigh of relief to have salvaged such a
reliable affection from the romantic wreck of my twenties.
Never underestimate the seductive powers of contentment.

There were times when I was sure we could do it, that we
would be one of those couples who survive and prosper.
There were times when he did the perfect thing at the right
moment. That night at the Majestic Hotel, for example.

In the September of our first year together, the Agency sent
me to San Francisco, to a very dull conference on Superfund
liability law and its possible implications for nuclear spills.
(The Agency was always very concerned with its future liability, even though a great deal of my time was spent writing
papers and press releases and newsletters that explained how
miniscule the chances of 'accidents' were. Even in the wake
of Three Mile Island and Chernobyl, many of my colleagues
were true-blue believers in nuclear power. Just as you can find
some naive souls who still feel Communism hasn't been
given a fair try, you could discover in the Agency's beige
hallways any number of trusting hearts who felt that clean,
efficient nuclear energy could save the world, if only those
hysterical environmentalists would stop their picketing and
listen to logic. I was always glad that I left the Agency before
they figured out whose sorry backyard would be hosting all
that radioactive garbage. We criticize government for moving
so slowly, but when you consider the people who go into it,
perhaps that's a good thing.)

Philip came out to California to join me for the weekend. I
had fallen hard at first sight for San Francisco. It is one of
those rare American cities where you meet beauty at every
turn, where geography and architecture have had the happiest
of marriages. I loved it all: the jangly neon of Chinatown and
the patrician grace of Pacific Heights and the gritty bohemian
sangfroid of the Haight. I loved my hotel, a serene old

Victorian lady perched on the crest of Sutter Street before it dips into Japantown. The Majestic has high old beds and wooden elevator doors that are painted with monkeys cavorting in the dress of seventeenth-century courtiers. There is a bar hung with black velvet cases of peacock-blue butterflies. The whole place smells deliciously of eucalyptus wood and the linseed oil they polish the furniture with. Life would be perfect, I felt, if only I could live at the Majestic forever and walk miles and miles with the salty fog in my face.

I was so at home in San Francisco that I dreaded that Philip wouldn't feel the same way, but he turned out to be a perfect traveling companion. He had come equipped with map and guidebook, but was willing to wander if I wanted to. He insisted on taking me to a fancy North Shore Italian restaurant his first night there, but was happy to picnic in our room the second night on crusty sourdough bread, camembert, Danish ham, and a bottle of Merlot. He seemed boyish and relaxed. For the first time since I'd known him he didn't have an air of checking his watch or worrying about a filing deadline.

On Sunday we drove up to Muir Woods. I was overawed by the prehistoric trees and the perpetual shade they cast. In such a setting you prize human companionship. Philip, whose turn of mind was far more scientific, marveled and took pictures. We stopped at a roadside inn for dinner.

'Do you ever wonder what other lives you could have lived if it weren't for this one? If you had ten lives to live at once?' he asked me over coffee.

'You mean, if I were a great singer or actor or something?'

'No, more the lives you, your present self, really could live, alongside the one you do live. The ones that would also fit your personality and tastes. What I mean is, I could *see* myself living here, working with a small firm, going to Carmel or Santa Fe for the weekends.'

'It's true, this place doesn't seem like a vacation spot.'

'So you could see yourself here too?'

'I say yes. Who wouldn't, after an afternoon like this one? But I wonder how much an Easterner, a true Easterner, could ever feel at home out here. We would always be expatriates.'

'So many people in California are from somewhere else.'

'But what makes them happy seems to be forgetting where they came from and starting fresh. Maybe you and I wouldn't be very good at that.'

He sighed, as if remembering his desk piled high with papers, the pleasureless social obligations, the centuries of Traynor history and the invisible expectations that went with it. I felt sorry to have brought that sad and responsible look back into his eyes. His thoughts had been sailing free as a hawk, and I had reminded him that he was a fly in amber.

'Then again,' I said, 'why couldn't we? What's stopping us?'

'Nothing, I guess. It's nice to dream, anyway.'

On the way back in the car we played a word game he had taught me. He won a neck-and-neck round with the word 'epoch', and good humor was restored.

We packed, made love in a slapdash, easy way and fell into a happily tired sleep. I was dreaming that we had missed our plane when a shifty, uncomfortable sensation woke me up. The bed seemed to be sliding slightly under us. I looked to see what time it was, and the lit numbers on the bedside clock were jiggling. The bedspinning feeling made me wonder if I'd had too much Merlot. Then I realized that what you joked about when coming to this town was actually happening. This was a tremor, or a quake – I was too scared and disoriented to tell which. I didn't want to wake Philip. I had some crazy idea that if I shut my eyes and pretended the room wasn't shaking it would go away. I simply pressed my palms flat against the mattress and prayed for the room to stay still. Just then Philip turned over and took me in his arms.

'It's just a tremor,' he said. 'I'm sure of it. It'll be over in a minute.'

The floor and ceiling did one more little shimmy, then settled back down. The clock was steady again. But I was still braced for disaster. Philip must have felt the tenseness in my legs and arms. Tired as he was (for he had worked every night the week before to get time free for this trip), he did not drift to sleep and leave me to my chickenhearted insomnia. He kissed me and stroked my hair and told me stories of how he used to go around campaigning with his father and the odd things people would give him, from homemade peach preserves to a complete Lionel train set he still had.

The tremor was so minor that they didn't even mention it on the morning news the next day. When we got home, Philip gave me a fisherman's sweater I had yearned over in a shop on the waterfront but rejected as too expensive. He had gone back and bought it when I thought he was picking up embroidered Irish linen napkins for his mother. The sweater was intricately cableknit and deliciously warm, and every time I wore it I remembered Philip's calm tender voice in the dark on the night I thought the world was ending.

That trip became a touchstone for me, a proof of how good we could be together. We took other trips and learned that we traveled easily as a couple. None of the horrible extremes of my earlier romances surfaced, either on our travels or back home. We fell into an affectionate routine of cooking and sleeping and reading together.

One December evening, we were lying in front of Philip's fireplace with our arms around each other and his mother's heirloom quilt tangled between us.

He said, 'I could lie here forever.'

'Me too.'

'We really should get married one of these days.'

'I guess.'

'No, really,' he said. 'How many couples do you know who get along as well as we do?'

'We *do* get along.'

'So let's do it sometime.'

On the heels of this proposal had come ... nothing. I kept my little rent-controlled apartment on Porter Street, Philip kept his townhouse in Kalorama a few miles away, and we spent our weekends and two evenings a week together. From time to time Philip would mention our wedding as a distant goal, and I always seemed glad for it to remain that way. How was it that I didn't notice the slow climb down from that high point we reached in San Francisco? We hadn't gone further or deeper together: we'd leveled out instead. For months and months that even keel had seemed like contentment to me. Until lately. Lately, I'd fought a strange sort of panic, a panic like your first time on roller skates or a tremor in the night.

I was setting the table when Philip came in, using the key I'd given him. (He hadn't given me a key to his place, claiming I'd lose it.)

He kissed the back of my neck. In spite of the heat he looked as crisp and cool as he had that morning. The only difference was that his cuffs were turned back.

My air conditioner, a struggling little window unit, wasn't powerful enough to overcome the heat wave. But though the apartment was still too warm, he didn't mention it. I think he thought of his nights at my place as camping out.

'So what are you getting your father for his birthday?' he asked at dinner.

'I thought some angora-lined gloves for when he walks the dog on winter mornings.'

'Good idea,' he said. 'Tell me what my half is.'

'I'll just put your name on the card. You're not pitching in for his present when he barely speaks to you.'

My father could not forgive Philip for being a Protestant, the first Protestant in the family. A Presbyterian, worse yet.

We talked about the heat, about the unusually heavy tourist crowds that summer – Philip and I both hated tourists – and about a shop Philip had found to refinish a Queen Anne sideboard his parents were shipping him. I didn't want to admit that I had no idea what Queen Anne anything would look like. Then Philip did the dishes while I took a cool bath and washed the dust of the shop from my hair. I came back into the living room in my pajamas with my hair slicked back, wearing White Shoulders perfume, which is one of my mating signals, but he had spread official papers all over the sofa and didn't look up. It was one of those evenings when nothing was doing until his work got done.

So I pulled out an old Agatha Christie, *Murder on the Blue Train*, and sat in the armchair.

'Which case is it?'

'Seymour Greenbaum.'

Seymour Greenbaum was an orthopedist from Cherry Hill, New Jersey, who'd nearly pulled off a spectacular Medicare fraud. Philip was arguing clemency on the grounds of character, family, and the many old people in the community who loved their orthopedist in spite of everything. Seymour Greenbaum would wind up serving weekends in some country club. Everyone would be happy.

At ten o'clock Philip put away his papers and came over and kissed my neck. Then he unbuttoned my pajama top, kissing my breasts along the way. I pulled his undershirt off, and felt for that telltale sign he'd stopped thinking about the law.

It was too hot for niceties, too hot for anything but sweaty urgency. But he waited for me to ask him before he came inside me. He liked to hear me ask him. He always made me say it. When he was inside me he held still for a minute, looking at me. Only when I began to move did he take over, pounding hard. He wore the same absorbed, competitive look he had when playing tennis. Sometimes it worried me, how much work sex was for men. I did my part, but that was more elective. They were never off the hook.

Afterwards we lay together in the doze before sleep, listening to the whine of the air conditioner. Philip kissed my shoulder.

Chapter III

Frank Sinatra was blaring as I walked into my father's house:

> Come on toots
> Put on your dancing boots
> And come dance with me
> Romance with me
> What an evening for
> Some Terpsichore
>
> Pretty face
> I know a swinging place
> So come dance with me
> Romance with me
> On a crowded floor

The first thing I saw was the table in the front hallway, covered with a yellow paper tablecloth, groaning with presents. My brother Dom had obviously bought the cane with the duck's head he'd been talking about. The bulky, turquoise package tied with iridescent ribbon had to be from Cynthia, who specialized in frivolous gifts.

Propped against the back of the table was a painting of my mother – Francesca's contribution. She'd commissioned it from some back-of-a-magazine 'artist' who worked from photographs. My mother's skin was orange. The shadows under her eyes were blue. She was smiling widely, something she never did in real life because she was ashamed of her teeth. She'd have hated that painting, but my father would treasure it. My mother had barely stopped breathing when he'd started the canonization process. In another five years family memory would have transformed her from an unreliable parent and indifferent wife into Marmee from *Little Women*.

On the dining room table was a huge sheet cake wreathed in pink roses, inscribed in blue icing. As I moved to inspect it, I saw that the icing read 'We Love You, Mad.' Francesca was standing by the buffet, fanning out pink paper napkins. She was wearing a drop-waisted eyelet sundress so sweet-looking no grown woman should have appeared in it. Yet it suited her, with her dark hair pulled back in an Alice band, her big brown eyes, her slim, childlike arms.

'"We Love You, Mad?"'

She scowled at me.

'It was a mistake.'

'Could we smoosh over the M?'

'Everyone saw it already.'

I went and hugged her. She stood stiffly in the corner of my arm. Francesca was not a big hugger.

'The cake is really pretty. Lots of frosting. Can I have a corner piece?'

'Corner pieces are for the kids,' said Francesca, but I could tell it cheered her up a little to deny me something. 'You want me to go upstairs with you and give that dress a press?'

I was wearing a navy blue linen sheath with a low boat neck. It had, predictably, wrinkled on the subway. I had come close to crying, getting dressed for this evening. I, the least pretty of four sisters, knew that no matter how appropriate or festive I looked as I walked out the door, I would feel washed-out and rumpled next to my sisters, the way you feel when you've just gotten off a seven-hour flight. Most strangers would call me attractive, but my own family called me 'Stringbean' and referred to my looks in pitying, bemused tones, as you used to hear retarded children mentioned in the bad old days.

My sisters had that generous Continental beauty which looks even better if the hair gets messed up, the collar button comes undone, the face glows. Francesca, Annette and Cynthia all had thick, slightly wavy hair, pale olive skin that didn't burn, and wide Italian mouths with beveled lips. They also had figures, *real* figures, like Sophia Loren's or Anna Magnani's. Classic big-busted, small-waisted figures, the kind that never go out of style with men.

I was flat-chested with long legs. I had my mother's white skin, dark hair and hazel eyes. I also inherited her widow's peak and air of melancholy. When I wore dark red lipstick, I looked a bit like a vampiress. My mother used to console me by saying I had a 'special' beauty all my own, but then my mother was also the person who promised me when I was fourteen that I would someday have cleavage.

'Linen is supposed to wrinkle,' I said to Francesca.

'If you say so. You're the clothes expert.'

'Where are Jerry and the kids?'

'They're out back. The kids were getting restless so Dad gave them some baby food jars to catch fireflies in.'

Those baby food jars could well have been left over from our childhood. My father, like most people who had survived the Depression, never threw anything away.

'Where's your boyfriend?' Francesca asked.

'He couldn't make it. Last-minute emergency at the office.'

Philip had called at six-thirty to tell me to go on without him. He couldn't hide the joy in his voice. He didn't realize

that sending me to my father's alone was like sending me into
battle armed with a slingshot.

It was hard to blame him. He just couldn't stand the noise
and chaos that swirled around the Campanellas. If the
Traynors were disturbed about something, they discussed it
quietly in the library after dinner. If they were depressed, they
became genteel 'problem drinkers' or tranquilizer addicts. If
they grew desperate, they quietly drowned themselves in the
lily pond, to be discovered by the servants the following
morning. Traynors did not make scenes.

'Dad's in the living room,' said my sister, dismissing me.

The living room was milling with paisanns, but the din was
manageable as yet.

'I told you to call for a ride,' said my father. 'Are you
crazy, walking in this heat?'

He was wearing a button-down blue poplin shirt with wide
short sleeves. All the old Italian men I knew wore such shirts.
He also wore a new pair of khaki trousers. There must have
been a trip to Sears with Francesca.

My father was still a handsome man, if heavy. His com-
manding nose and the fine line of his jaw and chin would
never be completely vanquished by fat. You could always see
a ghost of his youthful self. In his youth he'd looked like the
young Marlon Brando, and now he looked like the old Marlon
Brando. He smelled of Old Spice.

'Happy Birthday, Dad.' I had always refused to call my
father 'Daddy' as my sisters did. He wasn't that sort of father.

'So, the big businesswoman arrives an hour late,' said my
father. 'Swamped with customers, is that it?'

'Not exactly.'

My shop baffled and irritated my father, and he took it out
on me with such comments. My father had been raised to
believe that women who did not marry should be nurses, secretaries, or teachers, preferably parochial school teachers.

(Unlike many Catholic fathers of his generation, he did not want one of his daughters to be a nun, perhaps because that would leave her free to answer to a higher authority than his own. A nun would also present significant competition in the holiness contest. The habit and fifteen-decade rosary alone would give her an unfair edge.)

'You know, it's not too late to get a few skills under your belt. You've got typing, shorthand, you never have to worry,' he had said the day I bought The Second Time Around.

I patted his shoulder.

'Hey, Father,' said my father to the priest next to him. 'You remember my third one, don't you?'

Father Flynn nodded and smiled, but I was sure he didn't remember me. He was already doddering by the time I entered first grade at the Church of the Infant Martyrs parochial school. Now he spent his time pottering around the rectory and annoying the maintenance staff with his fussy questions about the church boiler and his insistence that the traffic bumps in the parking lot be repainted all the time.

'There's still some food left,' said my father, 'You go get some, you hear?' He turned away to discuss the new parish gym with Father Flynn. Then he turned halfway back towards me and said, 'This one's too generous for her own good. I hope you didn't go spending a lot of money on some foolish present.'

The living room was horribly hot. My father's neighborhood is an unfashionable cluster of 1930s houses that huddle behind the golf-course-like grounds of a huge insurance company, just over the District line. These pre-war houses never had central airconditioning, and we'd never had enough money to install it. Now, with a tidy retirement fund and the payoff on my mother's large insurance policy, my father could have afforded it. But he didn't want it. In his old age he was always a little chilly.

A big standing fan whapped away in a corner, blowing the women's skirts around and ceasing to have any effect if you moved more than five feet away from it.

I got myself a gin and tonic from the heavy mahogany sideboard that had been part of the set my parents bought on credit when they married. It was the first credit purchase ever in the Campanella family. My Italian grandparents believed strictly in the cash-down system. I leaned against the mantle, sucking a slice of lime and watching the groups of my father's friends, all talking at the top of their lungs, holding heavy glasses of Scotch or tumblers of Gallo red. No dainty little sherry glasses in this house.

My brothers and sisters would emerge from the crowd if I stood there long enough. It was better than plunging in to look for them and running the risk of encountering Cousin Josephina, Sister Mary Isadore, or other ghosts from the past. I recognized several old women I remembered from my childhood. They were the ones who sat in the back rows of the church every Sunday, wearing mantillas and carrying worn devotionals, the faithful souls who showed up even on rainy First Fridays. Suddenly a sermon of Father Flynn's came to mind, one in which he exhorted the women of the parish to continue wearing hats and mantillas to church even though Vatican II said they didn't have to. 'Remember,' he had intoned, 'you are dressing for Christ.' From a fashion standpoint I had to agree that it was a shame so few women wore hats anymore – but you had to be a real beauty to carry off a mantilla.

There was barely room to set my drink on the mantle, where it jostled for space with a Sacred Heart of Jesus plaque, my parents' wedding picture, and a grainy newspaper photo of the Enterprise (the aircraft carrier my father had served on during World War II) displayed in a scratched lucite frame. There was also a gauzy head shot of my sister Cynthia which had been a leftover from the *Purrr* shoot (my father didn't know this); three bottles of holy oil (in case a crowd of people needed Extreme Unction suddenly); an old lamp of rose-colored glass with French courtiers dancing on the shade; a plastic crystal rosary our cousin the priest had had blessed by the Pope in 1964 (this resided in a cedar box lined with red velveteen); and, tucked into the gilt-framed mirror, a sheaf of Palm Sunday palms.

The noise and heat pressed me up against the brick of the fireplace, but even the brick was not cool tonight. I could smell a very faint whiff of urine from the corner of the carpet our long-gone dog had often annointed. Then I saw my sister coming towards me through the crowd. It was like being stuck in an Alpine snowdrift and seeing a friendly St. Bernard bound towards you – just that feeling of delighted rescue, although Cynthia of course bore no resemblance to a St. Bernard. She was more like a dainty Siamese.

'I thought you'd never show up,' said Cynthia. She hugged me. Her hug is a real bone-crunching embrace.

'I almost *didn't* show up.'

'Who could blame you? What a zoo. Francesca is being impossible. After all these years of trying to boss me around she still hasn't given up.'

Cynthia's hair was redder and longer than it had been the last time I'd seen her. Her eyebrows were plucked to the delicate line that was the fashion that season. Her periwinkle eyes, large and keen, looked me up and down. Cynthia has the most intelligent eyes in the world, although somehow she is able to mask all that intelligence when she is vamping for the camera.

She looked impossibly fragile in a drifty chiffon dress printed with grey leaves and dull pink roses. I felt the pang of sorrow I always felt at her beauty, because I never could quite forgive her for it. I wanted to, I really wanted to. But every time I saw her, for that first minute envy rushed green to my heart.

'So where's Philip?'

'Working.'

'Couldn't take the family, you mean.'

'And Simon?'

'Still in New York. I waited for the afternoon train for him, that asshole. I barely had time to dress when I got here, and Francesca kept nagging at me to help her make the salad.'

'Can you imagine Simon in this crowd?'

'Let's not talk about him. If I talk about him I'll get too angry to enjoy the party. Besides, there's someone here I want you to meet.'

I was surprised. She was always introducing me to people in New York. We couldn't enter a coffee shop without seeing someone she knew. But here we were surrounded by old men speaking in the dialect of my father's little town in Campobasso, and old women with moles on their chins and rusty black silk dresses.

As if in answer to my question, a man came up from the wings. He was wearing a crisp white Oxford shirt a little too big for him. It looked freshly starched. I was so overcome with the heat that I wanted to lay my hot forehead against his chest, against that snowy white cotton. The man's eyes were a dark grey-blue fringed with black lashes. His black hair curled in ringlets at the base of his neck.

'This is Harry Sandburg. He's the lawyer who got me those residuals on the Taco Town commercial. He's a genius,' said Cynthia.

'Not quite. All it took was a law firm letterhead,' said the man, who had one of those flexible, sandpapery voices you associate with the less fashionable boroughs.

'He only charged me fifty bucks, too.'

'Well, that was nice of you,' I said weakly, and cast an interrogatory glance at my sister.

She answered, 'I'm not *that* mad at Simon. I brought Harry along because he moved here last month. His firm transferred him to the Washington office and he doesn't know *anybody*.'

Harry smiled at me, despite this speech that made him sound like a charity case. He had the sort of sweet and sad smile some Jewish guys have. It radiated a wry self-deprecation in which there was nothing humble or cringing. He probably doesn't date Gentile women, I thought to myself. Well, what do you care?

'Harry's just divorced,' said Cynthia.

'I'm sorry.'

'Don't be,' he said, but I could see he still was. 'Actually, I'm separated. Four months until it's final.'

'And I told you about Diana,' Cynthia said in sepulchral tones. This meant she had described to him my stranded relationship, my business troubles, and perhaps the time I had fainted from nervousness in the middle of a Brazilian pole dance at the Infant Martyrs spring pageant.

'We need drinks,' said Cynthia, and went off to find some. She shouldered her way through the crowd. She made it as far as the living room doorway, where she was collared by Mrs. Lesniak, the parish charismatic. Mrs. Lesniak spoke in tongues, and when she wasn't speaking in tongues, she liked to talk about it. I watched her smother Cynthia in her powdery embrace; she left a faint white streak on Cynthia's right shoulder. It served Cynthia right. She was always leaving me alone with eligible men (or men she believed were eligible) without advance warning.

'Well,' I said to Harry. 'How do you like Washington?'

'Not bad,' he said. 'It's very different from New York.'

'My sister will worship you forever for those residuals, you know. She was deeply bitter when she kept seeing that spot and never got any checks.'

'Your sister is incredible.'

I was surprised, not because he'd called my sister incredible, but because he said it fondly and familiarly, not in the tone of awe men usually used in referring to Cynthia.

'She's so completely herself,' he said.

'That's true. It's a quality she shares with the rest of my family.'

He smiled. When he smiled his eyes became purely kind and intelligent. The knot that had been growing in my stomach since I walked in dissolved. The air around us turned quiet and cool, although the noise in the room grew louder every minute, like the constant gunning of a car engine.

'Let's sit,' said Harry, for the piano bench behind us had just been vacated by my uncles Jack and Tony, who were going down to the basement to inspect a jigsaw my father had bought at a yard sale for twenty dollars.

We sat and talked about the heat, and how housing costs in Washington compared to those in New York. There was really nothing extraordinary about him, other than that combination of blue eyes and black hair. He was of medium height, say three inches taller than my five-seven. The smile was worth waiting for, but no woman would ever gape at this guy as he walked down the street.

As I noticed all this with my brain, other organs of perception were reacting independently. Around us, a hundred people attempted to outtalk each other, yet I could hear every word Harry was saying as if he were whispering in my ear. The effects of hunger, I thought to myself. Fatigue. This damn *damn* heat.

'I didn't have dinner,' I said. 'Would you sit on the front steps with me while I eat?'

This was as brazen an invitation as I'd ever issued a man at a party.

'Sure,' he said, and followed me to the kitchen, where there were huge bowls and pots of everything that was more genteelly displayed in the dining room. He stood there while I dumped some meatballs, some thin-sliced Italian bread, provolone, salami, and green olives onto a plate.

'Want anything?'

'No, your sister started feeding me the minute I walked through the door.'

My father's kitchen was the most lovable room in the house. It hadn't been changed since 1940 – gas range, ceramic sink and diamond tile floor all original. In here, the noise dimmed down a little. The cooking smells soothed me. I always feel better in the presence of a lot of food.

We stole half a jug of Chianti and two coffee cups, since all the glasses were on the sideboard. We were just leaving with our booty when sounds of turmoil came through the swing door between the kitchen and the dining room. Francesca was herding everyone in for the cutting of the cake.

'Oh God,' I said.

'Do we need to be out there?' said Harry.

I speared a meatball with a toothpick and wolfed it down. My mother's ghost at my elbow told me it was unattractive to eat with so much appetite in front of a man. Shut up, Mom.

'We can leave after the singing.'

I cracked open the swing door. There were my brothers, tall swarthy Dominic and short, fair Joey. They were three sheets to the wind already. Cynthia and Francesca were bustling around my father, placing him at the head of the table, putting spoons in the three boxes of ice cream, lighting the candles. It always annoyed me that Cynthia, who had the same clear-eyed vision of my father as I did, turned into a Daddy's girl the second she got home.

My middle sister, Annette, was finding seats for the card-playing widows. Annette was as close to an all-American girl as you can get when you're half-Irish, half-Italian. Her hair was the gleamy gold you see on the bindings of old books, and her eyes were sea blue. She was cheerful and even-tempered, although in family brawls she could get down to it with the rest of us. She was wearing a pale pink A-line dress that looked like something out of a Gidget movie.

'Happy Birthday to you,' sang everyone but my brother Joey, who started to sing 'You live in a zoo' and was quashed by a glare from Francesca. It took a while to finish, what with everyone starting on a different key as usual. Joey's Irish tenor soared above the crowd.

Harry and I watched from the kitchen doorway as the first presents were opened. My father was at his most charming and jovial. He loved a crowd, a party, an audience. He told a great joke. Every present had its accompanying schtick. He tried to hand Dom's duckhead cane to Marty Caprisi, his best buddy from the old neighborhood. 'You need it more than I do, Marty.' He clapped on the Panama hat that Annette had gotten him.

Cynthia's present was a surfboard, with 'Waverider' written on it in sparkly script.

'I always wanted one of these,' said my father, and put it next to his chair where he looked at it frequently, beaming. He was incredibly tickled with it. Whereas who knew which kitchen drawer my gloves would be shoved to the back of by the time winter came.

I didn't want to watch him open my gift. I'd already noticed that Joey was wearing the yellow Venetian silk tie I'd bought my father the Christmas before. My dad was always giving my presents away to other people in the family. I had tried practical gifts – socks and umbrellas and bathrobes – and fanciful gifts, big glass paperweights and engraved fountain pens. Nothing succeeded. He would open my presents with a grunt and lay them aside. I had long ago accepted that I was not my father's darling child, but that didn't mean I had to wait there for the moment when it would be demonstrated to the whole gang.

'Come on,' I said to Harry.

We sneaked out the back of the house and around the side, through a dirt alley crowded with lawnmowers, wheelbarrows and shovels. I poured Harry a brimming coffee cup of Chianti and another for myself.

'Can I smoke?' said Harry. 'I borrowed a Marlboro from your uncle Frankie.'

'Sure.' I hadn't pegged him for a smoker.

'I do this twice a year,' he said, lighting up.

The meatballs were so tender they fell apart on my fork. The provolone was moist and delicately flavored and had some body to it, not like that mushy stuff that passes for provolone at the supermarket. Francesca must have gone to Litteri's. I rolled the cheese up in the salami and ate it with my fingers.

Harry smoked more Luckys while I worked on my food and gulped some wine. After a while, I was a little drunk. So I asked him the story of his life. He was lonely, and tired of being new in town. So he told me.

Chapter IV

'My family was really disappointed when I left my wife,' said Harry. 'If they could have, they'd have kept her and divorced me. You know the first thing my mother said when I told her we were splitting up? She said, "What did you do to her?"'

'But it wasn't all your fault, was it?'

'They said I should have been more patient. Nancy was cheating on me with a doctor who worked in the same research lab she did. I said, choose him or choose me. What else could I do?'

'And so…'

'She chose him.'

He spoke in that distant tone divorced people acquire when they've gone through the failure of their marriage so many times that they've reduced it to the chopped-up texture of hamster litter.

Harry's ex-wife was what he called a Protestant Jew. Her family had come over from Germany in the mid-1800s and had been achieving the American dream ever since.

'She always liked people to have credentials,' said Harry. 'To give her credit, it wasn't a money thing. Her family had had money for so long that it wasn't all she cared about by a long shot. She wanted a man with more drive.'

'That's what this doctor has?'

'They're like Pierre and Marie Curie.'

I pried the rest of the story out of him. Some people like reading about plane crashes or watching talk shows about mothers who sleep with their daughters' boyfriends. I like hearing lurid accounts of other people's breakups. It makes me feel less of an underachiever.

Nancy began her affair when Harry left his job as in-house counsel to a Fortune 500 company and joined the struggling firm whose Washington office he worked in now.

'I hated being corporate counsel,' said Harry. 'Ever have a job you hate?'

'Oh yeah. Sure. Until I bought in to my shop.'

'Then you know what I mean. God Almighty, I hated everything about this job. Every day I worked there I'd get these horrible headaches at four in the afternoon. But Nancy felt it was the right place for me to be. A stepping stone, she called it.'

As he talked, I realized that his ex-wife had been a true drip. She forced him to see experimental plays with no scenery except a few metal folding chairs. She had a brief fling with Unitarianism in which he was required to accompany her to potluck dinners with people who were unreasonably cheerful and vague in their beliefs. She became a vegetarian and wouldn't allow meat in the house, not even an occasional T-bone steak.

'Unitarians make me nervous,' I said. 'They're so damn serene.'

'Exactly. Now Catholics and Jews both know that if you're alive you're in for constant, crushing guilt.'

'Guilt makes you appreciate sinning. It spices things up,' I said, remembering what a miracle sex still seemed to me, that in minutes I could shed my strict Catholic girlhood along with my clothes. Turning, as Rupert Brooke said in a different context, like swimmers into cleanness leaping. Catholic girls may start too late, but we know how to make up for lost time.

When I wasn't having sex, of course, I was shadowed by guilt about having had it and about intending to have it again.

In short, Nancy was no fun, although I wasn't sure if Harry realized that yet. I got the feeling that if you'd opened the Sandburgs' connubial icebox, you'd have found bottled water, orange juice, rice cakes and a head of broccoli. Harry couldn't surprise Nancy with chocolates, because she was allergic to refined sugar, and he couldn't bring her flowers, because she sneezed at everything that grew. Instead, he gave her what she liked – arrangements of cacti, and tiny rock gardens under glass. She also had a turtle aquarium that consumed an enormous amount of time. It contained three large boxers named Bushmill, Jamison and Jack Daniels – names Nancy thought were cute. The forty gallons of water it held needed to be changed every month, a task usually delegated to Harry while Nancy was working overtime (or what he thought was overtime).

'Whatever else I might miss, I'll never miss those turtles,' said Harry.

You may wonder why he confided in me this way. But people always confided in me. Something about my face seemed to listen, one lover had told me.

'God, I'm babbling,' Harry said.

'You aren't babbling,' I said. 'Stay there.'

The dining room was deserted now. From the den I could hear the basso of my father's voice followed by gales of soprano laughter. It occurred to me that someday soon my father would have some new woman to take care of him. He needed that from women, and women are suckers for men who need them. This time around, maybe he'd actually get the mothering he had married for the first time.

I cut two huge pieces of cake, one from a virgin corner, each piece complete with a pink sugar rose.

'Tell me about your family,' he said when I came back.

Then he said, 'No, you take the one with all the frosting. I bet you like frosting,' and my heart melted.

'You know Cynthia.'

'Yeah, and I met Francesca at the door.' He didn't look as if it had been a warm welcome.

(Francesca had said to me in the hall, 'Who is that guy Cynthia invited? She could have warned me.')

'Francesca isn't very friendly to strangers. I'm sorry, Harry.'

'She looks unhappy,' he said.

'She's never *been* all that happy. We didn't have what you'd call a Bobsey twins childhood, and then she got pregnant when she was sixteen. The last girl you'd have expected. I mean, Francesca was the golden girl in school. The nuns just loved her. She used to win prizes for collecting change in milk cartons to convert the pagans.'

'Of course, that's just the kind of girl it would happen to,' said Harry.

My mother had resented her oldest daughter terribly, ever since the day the fourteen-year-old Francesca had poured Mom's Johnny Walker down the sink. When Francesca got pregnant, my mother shipped her off to St. Agnes, a home for wayward girls in northeast Washington. We were told to lie about it at school, to say that Francesca was visiting relatives of my mother's in Boston. Away on a visit – the convenient fiction maintained about pregnant girls since time began, the lie that fooled nobody. Annette and I sneaked over to see Francesca at St. Agnes once in a while. The Home had cinderblock walls that seemed to weep moisture. The long dark hallways were hung with posters about prenatal health risks, alternating with framed reproductions of Baroque madonnas. Francesca was to give up the baby for adoption, but once she saw him, she wanted to keep him. My parents weren't having her back in the house with a baby in tow. So she married the child's father, who'd wanted to marry her since the day they met. Jerry was from a huge Irish family, thirteen kids, and only death and natural disasters shook his easygoing parents. His anticipation of the wedding day by a mere nine months didn't bother them a bit, and he'd turned out to be a good husband and a better father.

Before she got pregnant, Francesca had had a scholarship to Johns Hopkins. She'd wanted to be a doctor. Now she worked in a doctor's office, running research studies on diabetic diseases of the eye.

'Who's the sweet-looking blonde?' said Harry.

'That's Annette. She's married to Paul, the tall guy in the yellow-striped shirt.'

'She seems nice.'

'She *is* nice. She's one of the nicest people I know.'

Men liked Annette. She was the sort of girl who played baseball with the boys and could nail someone out at third base as well as any of them. She and Paul camped, hiked and fly-fished together. Annette had never owned a pair of high-heeled shoes in her life. She could change a tire, fix a leaky radiator, and kill large spiders. Paul could have married any number of well-groomed, grateful girls, for he was handsome in the same dark Italian way my father had been, and his family was gentry in our parish. He had chosen Annette instead, to my parents' everlasting delight. My father had refused to attend Francesca's wedding, but he beamed when he gave Annette away.

'I'm not all that close to Annette, but she's there if I need her,' I said to Harry.

'Why aren't you close to her?'

'She's so normal. Her whole life is like a reproach to me.'

'That's how I feel about my sister. She's a podiatrist married to an investment banker. Two kids already. And what about your brothers? What's their story?'

'Dominic you met. He's an environmental scientist. He spends all day standing in a swamp or marsh or something outside Baltimore, studying the wetlands. He's very intense. And Joey, he's all the Irish side of the family. Always joking. He can charm the leaves off the trees. He manages an auto repair shop.'

'It's not as complicated with your brothers, is it?'

'No, you're right, it's not. No one compares us.'

'This guy you're seeing, is he like your brothers?'

I laughed. 'Not a bit. Cynthia told you about him?'

'Her actual words were that you needed someone to save you from yourself.'

'I need someone to save me from Cynthia. Um, this is a nosy question, but have you and she ever …?'

'Not even once.'

'With Cynthia everyone *tries*.'

I was feeling the Chianti. I was also feeling that it didn't matter what I said to him, that here somehow was a person with whom I couldn't put a foot wrong.

'I guess I was shellshocked after the divorce. Also, don't take this the wrong way, your sister is a wonderful girl, but she would give me an ulcer in a week. She likes drama. She wants someone she has to go through hell and high water with. Like Simon.'

'What do *you* want?'

'Someone I can talk to, excuse the cliche,' he said. 'You?'

'Someone who won't annoy the hell out of me.' It occurred to me that one of Philip's best qualities was his soothing aspect. If Philip were what my uncle Tony referred to as an object of art, he'd be a Japanese screen or a Greek vase. Of course, you can't expect much in the way of emotional return from a vase.

We sat there licking frosting off our fingers. We could hear the cicadas buzzing and the occasional car honking on River

Road. Inside, someone was talking about last week's poker game, and there was a burst of masculine guffaws.

'You know,' I said to Harry, 'this whole neighborhood used to be orchards and farms. There's one big old mansion off Little Falls Parkway that was a stop on the Underground Railroad.'

'Hard to imagine people having that kind of courage,' said Harry.

'You have courage,' I said. 'You left the place where you grew up, which is more than I did. That took guts.'

'Acts of desperation frequently look like they take guts,' said Harry. 'And there's a fine line between bravery and stupidity.'

'I should go,' I said.

'I'll drive you,' said Harry. 'If you want.'

Oh, those moments of decision. Those moments when you know that a certain yes will lead to other yeses.

'That would be lovely,' I told him.

We left without saying our goodbyes, which would have entailed a round of relatives to kiss, priests to metaphorically curtsey in front of, and explanations to make as to why I was disappearing early with a man no one had seen before that evening. I took the cowardly way out. Cynthia would understand, and Francesca never would. What else was new?

Harry had a rattling old M.G. He put the top down and the wind swept my sticky hair off my face and riffled Harry's curls. He played a Chet Baker tape. 'Sweet Lorraine', and 'Isn't It Romantic?' drifted into the hot night air. In front of my apartment Harry cut the engine and waited. I knew if I said nothing he would watch me in politely and drive off.

'Come up and have some lemonade,' I said.

We walked up the four flights of stairs. In my apartment, Harry paced around. He unbuttoned another button of his shirt. He looked disheveled and disoriented. He said nothing, just inspected the place as if he were looking for clues.

'It's a dump,' I said, remembering some of Philip's comments, such as, In this day and age most people have a microwave oven.

'It's not a dump,' Harry said. 'It looks straight out of the thirties. I like that. My God, your phone even has a rotary dial. I love those old rotary dials.'

My building was of the 'shabby grandeur' school, with the emphasis on shabby. It had been built in 1910, one of the first true apartment buildings on this stretch of Connecticut Ave., and not much had been done to it since. The hardwood floors in my apartment were practically bare, except for a worn Persian rug in the bedroom, a gift of the woman from whom I bought my shop. For summer, the beat-up old armchairs and saggy old couch were covered in ivory linen and fringed white cotton bedspreads I'd found for five dollars each at an estate sale. There were a few pillows in cabbage rose chintz, many photographs in pewter frames, a wrought-iron cafe table where I ate my meals, and five bookshelves, all painted white, one with a glass door. Books teetered on top of them, since there were always more books than shelf space.

I watched Harry take all this in. He didn't get that condescending grown-up look I was used to seeing on the faces of visitors, the look that said: a woman this age should really own more furniture.

'Sit down, Harry. You look awful. This heat's not easy to get used to.'

He sat down.

'Take off your shoes, why don't you.'

He took off his shoes. He had long narrow intelligent feet. He sipped his lemonade. He put it down on the side table and spilled some of it, then tried to mop it up with his sleeve before I saw it. Very nervous. I wondered how many women's apartments he'd been in since his divorce.

'You know,' said Harry after we had been sitting in a awkward silence a few minutes. 'I've gotten a lot of parking tickets in this town. Every time I turn around I get one. The last one I got, there was even time left on the meter.'

'It's the one thing the D.C. government is efficient at.'

'They watch those meters like a hawk.'

'They sure do.'

'And then of course, you're thinking, do I just pay up or do I fight it?'

'It doesn't do any good to fight it. You spend the whole day in traffic court.'

'You're right. It's not worth it.'

We sat silent again. Then he said, 'You know, I really talked a lot tonight. I haven't talked that much to any woman for a long time.'

The next minute we were kissing. I'd known from the shape of his lips that he'd be a good kisser, and he was. We kissed for a long time, getting used to each other. In the back of my mind, or rather the pit of my stomach, the voice of guilt and reason was reminding me that I already had a lover, that Philip would never understand a lapse like this, that I was diving off a cliff into a lake with hidden rocks under its surface. The voice droned on and on, like the noise of a far-off lawnmower when you're trying to sleep late. I ignored it. There would be hell to pay later, but right now I wanted just this, exactly this.

Sometime later I unbuttoned Harry's shirt. His chest hair smelled of some ferny aftershave and his own smell, which was like faint sandalwood. I sucked his nipples and he groaned, and then he couldn't find the zipper on my dress, because it was on the side. Then my dress was off and Harry was on top of me, there on the couch, kissing my neck.

I disentangled myself briefly to say, 'Harry, I should have brought this up before, but ... I know you've been married a long time, but have you, are you checked out?'

'Oh yeah,' he said. 'My father told me women asked that nowadays, so I went out and got it done.'

'Your father told you that?'

'My father is quite the ladies' man.' Then, as my fingers caressed his neck: 'Never mind. I'll tell you about him another time.'

He hadn't asked but I said, 'I'm all checked out too.' At which he smiled, a smile that made his eyes glow blue-green, and I realized that it was the sunburst of clear gray inside the blue iris that gave him the starry-eyed, dazzled look and lent his smile such warmth.

'You have such a pretty gray inside your blue eyes, Harry,' I whispered.

'No one's noticed that in twenty years,' he whispered back.

I could feel his five o'clock shadow rough against my skin. The roughness made me shiver even as hot as it was. I found his penis with my hand and it was painfully hard and I smiled, because it always feels triumphant, when you hold them for the first time and feel that hardness which says want, want, want and it's for you. I felt cocky then and took him in my mouth and hands, and when he groaned again I felt more, a passion of generosity because he had rescued me from the sweltering bosom of my family and brought me back to my own safe rooms. And just when I thought, what the hell I can wait, let's finish it this way, he pulled me up and somehow we adjusted ourselves and he was in me, below me with his hands on my waist.

I watched his face grow younger and younger, fierce and

young and concentrated. I moved on top of him. I tried to make it feel good, and then I was *sure* it felt good from the way he looked, and I tried to make it feel even better, and then I forgot about what I was trying to do. His fingers found the right places, and we were frantic together. At the end I buried my face in those dense springy curls and the last thought I had was how black they were against the ivory linen. That was the end of that time.

After a while I worried I was too heavy, and made to move, but he held me against him. He cradled my head in his big hands and whispered, 'Thank you.'

'Oh thank *you*,' I whispered back. We stayed like that for a long time, and then he said, 'Should I go?' and I said, 'Stay. If that's okay.'

We made a sketchy bedtime routine. He borrowed my toothbrush and splashed cold water on his face and chest. I staggered through the usual round of checking locks and making sure the gas wasn't on, washing my face, getting ice water to keep by the bed, changing into the cotton slip I like to wear when it's hot. It seemed to take us forever to settle down for the night. When we were finally in bed we lay flat on our backs, holding hands. The sky outside my window was so dense with humidity and pollution that it was dark brown with an orange haze at the edges.

'I don't usually do this sort of thing,' I told him. I was so exhausted and happy that I didn't even care if he believed me or not.

'Shh,' he said. Then he sighed and lifted the slip and climbed on top of me, and I wrapped my legs around him so tightly he couldn't have escaped if he wanted to. He was ardent, and more assured this time, and I let him have it his way with everything, since I'd had my way first.

At four o'clock the thunder woke us, so loud it seemed the windows would crack. We watched until the storm became a steady downpour. I opened the window that didn't have the air conditioner in it, and great draughts of cool air came into the room. Harry turned on his side and drew me to him. I fell asleep with the sweet fresh air on my face and his warm arm around me.

Chapter V

'So,' said Cynthia. 'How was last night?'

She had come by the shop, as promised, to see the new clothes.

'I think Dad had a good time.'

'You know what I mean.'

There was a silence, as my sister's McCarthyistic assumption that she had the right to know the details made itself felt. Usually I resist this pressure, but today I was guilty and confused. Sex, frantic soulshaking sex, leaves you hopelessly off your game.

'I slept with him.'

'Good for you! *Good* for you!'

'You sound like you're congratulating me on not having any cavities.'

'How was it?'

'It was fine.'

'Fine?'

'It was good.'

The silence again.

'It was great, okay? You're a sick person wanting to know these things, you know that?'

'This is vital information. You can't leave it out. It affects everything.'

'I told him this morning, it was a one-time thing.'

I had never had to tell anyone that before. I'd never had a one-night stand before. Thirty-two years old and I was having my first one-night stand. Why couldn't I have done this sort of thing fifteen years ago, when everyone else was getting it out of her system? I would always be out of step with my generation, which was now through with sexual experimentation and instead embracing exercise and abstinence or the marriage-and-mortgage routine.

Harry had looked more disappointed, more crestfallen, than I'd expected. I had sent him out into the sparkling summer morning as if he were some horrible barfly who had taken advantage of my inebriation. But having him there made me wild with guilt. I had shouted it down last night but this morning here it was, grown tenfold during its time in captivity. I had cheated on Philip, and it put me outside some moral pale I'd always stayed comfortably within before. In the past, when I'd had things to hide from him (such as how I felt about his lime-green golf sweater and some of his Hill rat friends), they had always been things I was pretty sure he wouldn't care much about anyway. This night with Harry was the sort of secret that fueled the plots of Victorian novels, the sort of secret you knew would undermine the heroine's brightest prospects, the sort that ended in her dying of consumption or drowning or some other suitably anguished fate.

'Look,' said Cynthia. 'Don't go embroidering scarlet letters on all your lingerie. If you slept with him, it was because you felt something.'

'I felt something all right.'

'Yeah, but you wouldn't have felt horny if you didn't genuinely like him. I know you. You're the queen of the cold shower. The woman who's left a trail of blue balls behind her.'

'I am a complete slut.'

'You stop that. Right now.'

'Well, what else would you call it,' I said. My shop was empty, the way it always was. I was a slut *and* a business failure, unlike the vixens on *Covington Heights* who could break up marriages and run multimillion-dollar industries and still have enough time in the afternoons to stop by the town dress shop and eavesdrop on important conversations in the changing room. My business wasn't even a business. It was a couple of rented rooms filled with other people's castoffs.

'Why do you have to call everything something?' said my sister. 'So you can classify what sort of sin it is? Okay, it's a mortal sin. Like every other thing that's pleasant in this world. Come on. You probably made Harry feel more appreciated than he's felt in years. And it's not like he's any danger to you or Philip. He hasn't been with more than one or two women since his divorce.'

'He told me he had all his shots, so to speak. That doesn't change what I did. I betrayed Philip the worst way you can betray someone.'

Her voice softened, the cue that she was about to give me advice. Cynthia dispenses advice only to people she really cares about. The rest of the world she simply observes with a jaundiced eye. You don't become a sex goddess without getting a little cynical.

'Look, honey, Philip is dragging his feet. You can keep putting up with it or you can go out and find someone who'll treat you the way you deserve.'

'I could say the same to you about Simon.'

'Yeah, but we aren't talking about me.'

The bell jingled and a tourist came in. If you have lived in Washington your whole life, you can spot a tourist at three hundred yards. This woman, a little heavy, a little jowly, was wearing shorts in a tropical print with a matching blouse and enormous, overproduced sneakers. She was carrying a plastic bag from the Air and Space museum and another plastic bag from which a t-shirt depicting the Washington monument was sticking out. I wondered how she had wandered so far up this way.

She was puffing from the stairs but smiling, wanting conversation. I smiled back. Then she looked around and her expression changed.

'Isn't any of your stuff new?' she said.

'No, I'm afraid not,' I said.

She fingered a few jackets, doubtfully. Among them was the French blue vintage one I had set aside on a hanger for Cynthia. The brown and black check had sold long ago.

She said, 'I thought you had new. An old friend of mine told me about this place. She didn't say it was secondhand.'

'Well, it is,' I said coldly.

'I just have a thing about wearing secondhand,' she said. She eyed a few scarves and gloves, then retreated back down the stairs.

When the door chimes had jingled again, Cynthia said, 'Why did you treat that woman that way?'

'What way?'

'As if she smelled.'

'Did you see how she handled that jacket? It would've been way too tight for her anyway.'

'Couldn't you have said, no, my stuff isn't new but I have the finest designer wear? Couldn't you have shown her that whole rack of Liz Claibornes? They were just her style.'

'She wanted new, she could go find new somewhere else.'

'Look, Diana, are you running a museum or a store here?'

'People just don't admire good workmanship anymore. Look at the hem on this skirt. Lace-basted. By hand. She wants new, she can go to a department store and buy some cheap synthetic with stitches as wide as my hand that will fall apart in six months.'

'I know. It's a tragedy. Unfortunately, if you don't start

selling to some of these philistines, you're going to be out of business and back at the Agency before you know it.'

She had found the talking point. The nightmare that woke me up at three a.m. was returning to the Agency with my tail between my legs. It would be mean going back to the whole deadly routine: those mornings on the subway, hating all the other people on the train: the men with their too-short fifties haircuts and briefcases. The *women* with their too-short fifties haircuts and briefcases. The way black people looked at the white people, and white people looked at the black people. If there had been barbed wire and trenches between us we couldn't have been further apart.

And then the Agency itself. The shuddering fluorescent lights. The stacks of old Federal Registers piled everywhere like tiny Towers of Babel. The coffee that tasted like brake fluid no matter how often you scoured the pot. The defeated ranks of my fellow workers. The men's shoes were never polished. The women had the discouraged, dowdy air women get when they know no one will notice them even if they look like Grace Kelly. Juiceless, sexless, beaten down by procedure – that was what people became at the Agency.

At the Agency, we were issued security passes to wear on chains around our necks. We sat in endless meetings where technocrats suggested ideas such as ferrying spent plutonium down the East Coast in barges and across the Panama Canal to reach its final destination, which was burial on some Indian reservation in Washington State. As if we hadn't already done enough to the Indians. My job was to ghost-write articles and speeches for department bigwigs about the safety of nuclear storage casks and the progress the Agency was making in finding a place for all this deadly flotsam and jetsam of progress.

I worked there four years, and when I left people thought of me as having been a short-timer. Only four years, when most of them left by retiring or through intervention by the Grim Reaper. People at the Agency were like lifers at a minimum security prison.

The glorious, highly-colored world beckoned outside, but day by day they believed in it less and less.

As in the slammer, there weren't many events at the Agency to break up the time. There was the annual Christmas party at some Ramada Inn in Crystal City or Gaithersburg (just when I'd thought the last one couldn't get any worse, someone had brought in a karaoke machine). And the fall and spring blood drives that separated the men from the boys, so to speak – I gave every time and always fainted over my post-donation orange juice and cookies. Even the Thanksgiving potluck was predictable. You knew what everyone would bring and what would be left over. Barb Steinmuller's sweet potato pie with graham cracker crust always remained virginally unsliced, while Charlie Reardon's sausage-and-chive stuffing disappeared twenty minutes into the festivities.

When I left, my supervisor, Mr. Moriarty, told me that he would do his best to find a spot for me whenever I wanted to come back. They threw me a farewell lunch at one of those big Tex-Mex places down by the river and gave me a day planner with my name stamped in gold on the cover. As I drove away in the cab, I saw them all straggling back to the office, and felt like a paroled prisoner after the Warden says, 'Good luck out there, Joe. Let us know how you do,' and the gates clang behind him.

'I don't want to go back there,' I said to Cynthia. 'But I don't know what to do with this place.'

'You could start with some changes. Like decent bags,' she replied.

'What's wrong with the bags I'm using now?'

'They're plastic. They look cheap. Half of retail is romance. The bag is your image. Do you want your image to be thin plastic? If you love these clothes so much, why not send them away in a bag that does them justice?'

'Mary always used plastic.'

'Mary had a husband who was a GS 15, as I remember. Mary didn't need a job. She needed a place to go in the mornings.'

In the next hour, while we waited for *Covington Heights* to come on, Cynthia roamed through The Second Time Around with a yellow legal pad, noting flaws.

'These booths are like stables. Even Filene's has doors on their dressing rooms.'

'I can't afford fancy dressing rooms, Cynthia.'

'Fancy-looking, not fancy-costing. You could afford curtains for instance. We could make them ourselves. Or just layers and layers of gauze draped over a pole.'

'That's right, gussy up the place just as I'm going out of business.'

'You have to gussy it up to save it. Women don't shop like men, you know. Men shop with tailors crawling up their inseam and the salesman suggesting a bigger waist size right in front of everyone. But women are very self-conscious. Your fortyish career woman doesn't want to stand out in the open at the same mirror with some perky young thing in a mini-dress.'

'But then I have to have mirrors and lighting in every cubicle. It'll cost a fortune.'

'Trust me,' said my sister. 'We can do it for under a thousand.'

'I only have five thousand left.'

'Exactly why you need to spend a little. And why does this tag say: "Vintage: Handle With Care"? Who's going to try it on if they think they'll get sued for sweating on it?'

My head was reeling. Cynthia was waltzing around my private sanctuary, laughing at my sacred objects.

I never showed my family anything I cared about. I'd learned better a long time ago. They believed that being related to someone was a license to hold him or her up for ridicule. Whoever wrote, 'Love means never having to say you're sorry,' could have been describing them. For example, when I was thirteen and my mother bought me my first training bra (which I didn't need) my sister Francesca sneaked that bra out of the back of my drawer and tied it to the handle of her bicycle. Her subsequent tour of the neighborhood, with the tiny white flag on display, was one of those childhood memories the Hallmark people just don't make a card for.

'Did I ask for your advice?' I said to Cynthia.

'No, but if there's one thing I know, it's shopping. You've got a choice. You can operate a little hole in the wall for a few other people as cheap and eccentric as you, or you can turn this place into something hip and inviting that any passerby will want to stroll into.'

'Stroll into. Right. I'm on the second floor.'

'Well, then, we'll do a window display. That shoe repair place down there doesn't need the window. It's full of dirty old shoes. You're going to have to do something about that. Tell them you'll take it and in return pass out their coupons or whatever. You could be a good source of business for them.'

I felt as if some marine drill sargeant had stripped me down and was laughing at my poor muscle tone. At the same time, some internal fog was lifting and a golden misty light was peering though it. She made sense, and I couldn't possibly, possibly do worse with the place than I was doing. I was three months away from shutting down.

But Lord, it was hard to take advice from my dashing little sister. Bad enough to be always the cautious one, never the adventurous one. Cynthia left home at seventeen to conquer New York City. She'd done singing telegrams, taught aerobics at rich people's penthouses, danced topless in Tokyo, modeled lingerie in Milan showrooms. She could tell stories of the night markets in Hong Kong and the time she had scared away a mugger in her lobby. Next to her, I felt spineless and circumspect.

'You should change the name, too. The Second Time Around just screams used clothes. What you want is a cool shop that just happens to be secondhand. You know, like American Rag in San Francisco or Renaissance Garage in Soho.'

In the midst of this orgy of improvement, we stopped to watch *Covington Heights* on the tiny black-and-white television I kept in the back room. Charmaine was now planning to poison the family housekeeper because the housekeeper had noticed that Charmaine wasn't allergic to artichokes the way Simon's real wife had always been. Luckily for Charmaine, the family housekeeper was already taking digitalis for a heart condition. Such a simple thing to increase the dosage and put it down to an accident! Meanwhile, Brice was shown discussing his doubts with his devoted twin brother Edwin (who was also played by Simon, through some miracle of television). While Brice affected a brooding look and a lord-of-the-manor wardrobe that ran to ascots and smoking jackets, you could tell Edwin by his pullovers, mussed hair, and sneakers.

'You love her, don't you?' Edwin asked Brice. Edwin had just fallen in love himself with *Covington Heights'* only female tycoon, pantyhose heiress April Dunning. Edwin believed in love, but he didn't have a chance with April. April was in love with the chief of police, who used to run a rock club and had been made police chief with no discernible qualifications (other than having saved April's life after a freak spelunking accident). We all knew that Edwin was going to wind up with Conchita, the Nicaraguan maid who had such a crush on him and was really a Federal agent in disguise. I was rooting for Conchita. I always rooted for the brunette over the blonde.

'It's so wonderful having Olivia back with me, home where she belongs,' said Brice to Edwin, 'but I can't shake this feeling that something terrible's going to happen. And Mrs. Moultrie is acting so oddly!'

The camera cut to Charmaine making a pot of coffee for the doomed Mrs. Moultrie. As she poured the liquid and dropped the pills in the cup, the music came up. A commercial for disposable diapers appeared, with a baby who danced because he didn't have diaper rash anymore. The baby wasn't even cute. It was too skinny, not chubby and round like babies should be. Maybe they kept these commercial babies deliberately uncute, so as not to threaten mothers with skinny little babies who looked like plucked chickens.

'Is Mrs. Moultrie really going to die?' I asked Cynthia. Mrs. Moultrie gave me a pain. Here she was, sixty, still working for this inconsiderate rich family that apparently hadn't even thought to offer her a pension and a nice long cruise for all her years of devotion. All she did was hang around offering people cookies and making concerned remarks in a bogus Irish accent.

'She's a goner,' said Cynthia. 'They just don't know what to do with her anymore. Simon told me. I talked to him last night.'

'What's the latest about Delia?'

'She's on Prozac now. It's making *her* a lot happier but it isn't speeding up the divorce any. Now she has this idea she's going to become an interior decorator.'

'Cynthia.'

'I know, I know. But he gets these tears in his eyes whenever I talk about leaving him.'

I had seen those tears. So had half of the women in

America. The poor guy probably couldn't get up to go to the men's room without a three-curtain farewell speech. His emotional seismometer must be fatally offkilter after all these years playing Brice Covington. At last count, Brice had lost three wives, a fiancee or two, several businesses, and (temporarily) the ability to walk. This would be enough to encourage the brooding streak in any man, let alone an actor.

'So Simon's tears are worth more than your tears?'

'Just shut up, okay? If I want to talk to Alex, I'll call Alex.'

Alex was Cynthia's shrink back in New York. When Cynthia was in crisis, she turned to Alex or Surnami, her personal astrologer. She never turned to me, her big sister. Not for advice, anyway. My role was the patient listener, the admiring encourager, the reliable port in a storm. There is a poem by Robert Frost that goes, 'The heart knows of no devotion/ greater than being shore to ocean.' Well, that was okay for the one who was the ocean. Not so hot for the shore.

'Definitely, change the name,' my sister told me before she left. 'In fact, let's close down for two weeks and reopen. The whole place needs a face lift.'

'Close down? Whose business is this?'

'Yours. But I need a project. I can't hang around the family mansion all day. Daddy will drive me crazy.'

'Daddy? Who's *your* father? Was it Mr. Pelter after all?'

Mr. Pelter was our childhood milkman.

'Admit it, Diana, you could use the help.'

'I'll think about it.'

'Think about Harry, too. By the way, I called him this morning and told him not to give up on you.'

'Cynthia!'

She ran down the steps laughing, the light graceful run earned by several years of classical ballet training my mother had paid for out of grocery money. Shore to ocean, indeed.

Cynthia was an enormous wave that crashed over me, shoved sand and salt up my nose, and deposited me gasping on the shingle. And yet...*Cynthia's*, I thought to myself. A one-word name. A name that wasn't about anything. It was simple and elegant and would look good on those new bags.

Chapter VI

Cuisine Grandmere sounded as if it should be cozy, but it wasn't. The tables were cold green steel and glass, so you could see your lap as you ate. The interior walls were squares of frosted glass that looked like stacked ice cubes. Through these cubes ran veins of neon tubing in which the colors were constantly shifting. The effect was a cross between the inside of an aquarium and the United Airlines terminal at O'Hare.

The food was trendy and eclectic. One of those places where you had to have a culinary degree just to know what the ingredients were.

I wore a dark red scoop-necked dress that Philip had always liked, with heavy silver earrings. My hair was drawn back in a chignon, a style Philip had once referred to as 'classic.'

'You look pretty tonight,' he said. 'That red sets off your hair.'

We smiled at each other. A waiter arrived. He seemed astonished that we had been allowed in the door. Waiters in excellent Washington restaurants are trained in this snooty expression, and we were too far uptown for any restaurant to know who Philip was. When we ate down on Capitol Hill it was like old home week. There everyone had known Philip since he was ten.

The food didn't justify the waiter's obnoxiousness. The

vinaigrette on my salad tasted like the vinegar had gone off.
The vegetable root bread had stringy bits of root in it. And the
air was frigid, as if the walls really were frozen blocks of ice.
While Philip engaged the waiter in a long and complicated
discussion about what kind of wine we should have with his
veal in boysenberry sauce and my tangerine duck, I sat and
shivered.

'My mother says hello,' said Philip, as we sipped our
drinks.

His mother never really said hello. I'd once heard him ask
her on the phone, 'Should I say hello to Diana for you?'

Needless to say, his family wasn't thrilled about me. I was
half-Italian, and Catholic even if lapsed. I didn't dress in the
political wives' uniform of dowdy suits with knee-length
hems, jewel-neck collars, loudly patterned silk scarves and
low Mamie Eisenhower heels. Sometimes I appeared in a
short black dress or stockings with a back seam. Or a poet's
blouse with tight velvet pants, or a pair of rose and white chiffon slip dresses, one over the other. No one wore these sorts
of clothes in the Traynors' world.

The women in Philip's family were what used to be called
'womanly women'. They were skilled in the domestic arts,
the civic virtues, and the sociable sports. They had great back-
hands, learned to waltz at the age of eight, and thought it the
height of fun to create seasonal wreaths for their front doors.
They could crochet and knit and embroider. Each had a hobby
such as making dolls from pinecones or arranging dried flowers under glass. They could ride, of course, and liked dogs. I
spooked horses and was afraid of dogs, ever since I was eight
and a golden retriever bit me on the neck at Maureen Santini's
confirmation party.

Philip's parents did not know what to make of me, yet they
were growing resigned. Having Philip end up with me was
better than his remaining a bachelor all his life. Back home in

Montville, there were two types of bachelors: the type who were suspiciously cultured and artistic, and the type who were tacitly understood to be 'odd' – the word 'odd' covering everything from exhibitionism to sitting up late at night making model airplanes. To see Philip escape either of those classifications was certainly worth admitting a little foreign blood into the family.

I know, I know. This is America, and I should have gotten over feeling as if, when we went to see Philip's family at their limestone mansion out in Chevy Chase, I should go round to the servants' entrance. But somehow I had conned myself into believing that Traynors were doing me a favor, letting me sit at the same dinner table with them.

Meeting Harry had put a lot of new thoughts in my head. As I sat demurely opposite Philip and tried to avoid choking on some sort of turnip fiber in the bread, it occurred to me that I had something of my own to offer his snobbish clan. Didn't every old family need a few newcomers to give them vitality and perspective – that great immigrant determination, free of inbreeding, full of stamina? Whatever quality enabled peasants who had never left their village to pack up their few things, cross the unknown ocean, and endure the sweat and humiliations of the New World, it had to be more priceless than Mrs. Traynor's great-great Aunt Lucinda's cruddy old sampler. Surely Philip's family, which had lived on Easy Street since America had paved roads, could do with a little infusion of proletarian energy?

Another point that should have counted in my favor: when it came to the money angle, my heart was pure and disinterested. I rarely allowed Philip to pay for dinner or movies. I contributed my half to the weekend at that bed-and-breakfast in Harper's Ferry, the night at that inn in Annapolis, the five-day trip to Cape May last September. At Christmas, my gifts made up, in ingenuity and number, for Philip's more expensive, conservative choices. For example, our first year together I found a set of perfectly matched Victorian pale blue and pink hand-tinted ceramic cups, perfect to hold his toothbrush and shaving brush, and a box of blown-glass 1920s ornaments at Tallulah's, a little shop in Takoma Park. I added a pair of navy silk boxers from Victoria's Secret, a big painted tin cannister of home-made candy cane cookies, and a bottle of Dom Perignon. Then I wrapped every gift in white and silver tissue with real satin ribbons, and put them in a huge red velvet stocking I'd made out of a remnant I'd found at Exquisite Fabrics down on K Street. He'd been delighted – as I'd been delighted with the cashmere scarf and sweater from Neiman Marcus, the engraved pen, and the boar bristle hairbrush to replace the dimestore plastic one he hated to see me use.

Not only did I insist on paying my way and reciprocating in the gift department, I was good for the long haul, too. No man would ever have to worry about supporting me. My shop was to me what a longed-for child would have been to another woman, and I would never give it up. If it failed, I'd find other work. That's what women in our family did; it was in our blood to toil. Philip was no meal ticket to me, and you'd think his parents would appreciate that and show some enthusiasm for my self-supporting if struggling little business. But the last time I'd seen them, Mrs. Traynor had said (with a tone in her voice that was the verbal equivalent of raising a lorgnette), 'And how is your shop, er, Time After Time, doing? Do you get many donations?' as if I were a Saturday volunteer at the Junior League shop.

'Consignments, Mother,' Philip had said absently, and the subject was dropped while Senator Traynor told us the story of how he had blocked the building of a discount mall that had threatened a very exclusive section of Mobile. Senator

Traynor always looked confused when I appeared at the house with Philip, as if I were some constituent he'd seen once, made some vague promises to, and had expected to go away. Once he called me 'DeeDee' by mistake.

Someday, I dreamed, I would casually pick my teeth with the butter knife at the end of one of Mrs. Trayor's elaborate repasts. Or fondle her darling son under the table. Or pull out a bottle of Cherry Snowcone nail polish and start painting my nails in the middle of one of the senator's longwinded tales about LBJ. Someday, I would not care what they thought of me. That day was not now, but somehow my evening with Harry made it seem a little closer.

Harry had called earlier that afternoon.

'I just wanted to tell you I had a really good time last night.'

'So did I,' I said, cringing as I remembered my fever of guilt that morning, the way I'd shoved him into his pants and immediately retreated to the shower. I was engaged, even if tepidly engaged, and I had done something that I'd never thought I would do: cheated. All these years I thought I'd coped magnificently with defying the rules of my girlhood. I had had sexual congress with Protestants while still unmarried. I had eaten hamburgers on a Friday, even though I had to choke them down. I hadn't been to Mass on a non-holiday Sunday since college. And now it seemed that this one transgression with Harry had roused the ghosts of every glacial nun, every thundering priest, every prig like my sister, that I had ever banished. I had made up my own moral code to replace the old Baltimore Catechism, but all along the Voice of Retribution had bided its time, waiting for me to slip up in some way even I couldn't ignore. Never underestimate what really competent brainwashing can do to your moral compass. Mine could not distinguish between a harmless fling and murder in the first.

'I was thinking,' said Harry in his croaky voice. 'Is there any reason we can't see each other again?'

An immediate pull of temptation, filings to a magnet.

'We talked about this already.'

'Yeah, but I was still half-asleep. That wasn't fair.'

'I know that Cynthia called you.'

'Yes, actually.'

And I could imagine what Cynthia had said to him: 'Diana really likes you. Normally you have to pry her knees apart with a crowbar. Her boyfriend's a spoiled aristrocrat who will never marry her. Keep trying.'

Strangers on a Train is playing tomorrow night at the Kennedy Center Film Institute, what do they call it, the AFI,' said Harry. 'Have you ever seen *Strangers on a Train*?'

I had not. One of my lifelong ambitions was to see on the big screen every film Alfred Hitchcock ever made.

'As long as this isn't a date,' I said.

'Okay.'

'And you won't try to hold my hand.'

'No hand holding.'

'And if you lunge at me at the door of my apartment building, it's understood that I'll have to knee you in the groin.'

'I've never lunged at a woman in my life,' said Harry. 'But if it makes you feel any better, I can sit five rows behind you.'

I'd have put Harry in perspective by tomorrow night, I figured. The man hadn't been invented who couldn't be fit into his own particular pigeonhole. Even Philip had his pigeonhole: reliable lover with cold feet.

Now I sat opposite this reliable lover, on whom I had cheated twelve hours earlier. Philip was chewing his first piece of veal with that listening look upper-class people have when they take their first bite of game or first sip of a fifty-dollar wine.

He apparently was satisfied, because he rested his fork on

the edge of his plate, a sign that he was about to say something. This was another difference between us. It was hard for me to let go of my silverware once I was eating. I still had to restrain myself from gripping my knife and leaning over my plate as if someone were going to take my food away. Cynthia calls this eating style 'the immigrant hunch'.

'I've been doing some thinking,' said Philip. 'You seem to be getting pretty restless. You're always wanting to work late, you spend all your free time with Cynthia. You almost never go with me to office functions anymore.'

'I told you how I felt about those. Once they find out I'm not a lawyer, I may as well be one of the waiters for all the attention they pay me.'

'But you used to do that sort of thing just to support me in my work.'

'Well, I don't see you coming to my shop and tagging new arrivals.'

'There's no comparison.'

I scraped orange marmalade off my duck and waited. Somehow I knew that if I apologized now for nonexistent sins against him and his holy law firm I would never regain the ground I'd lose.

'I don't want you to leave me,' said Philip. 'We're a great team.'

A great team. You give a man some of the most profound moments of your life, and he tells you you're a great team.

'And I have a feeling,' he continued, 'that if we don't get married you may start to think about ending this.'

'Did I say that?'

'No, but it's the natural conclusion. Then there's Cynthia, always encouraging you to leave me.'

There was a pause while the waiter, earning his tip, refilled our water glasses, tweaked the wine in its silver basket, and eyed disapprovingly the mess I'd made with my breadcrumbs. He was one of those angelically beautiful gay men, beautiful in a way straight men never are. The perfection of his features made him appear unsuited to his job, a sneering Latvian prince disguised as a waiter.

'I want you around and I always will,' Philip said after the waiter left.

'Why?'

He had to think.

I said, 'Because you're comfortable with me?'

'I've grown accustomed to your face.'

He smiled, the boyish smile I'd always loved. He held my hand. There are hidden springs of freshness in any love; sometimes they bubble up just when you think the well's run dry.

Philip had told me a story once about the day men had come to lay linoleum in his mother's kitchen, or rather, his mother's servants' kitchen. Coincidentally, it happened to be on the day of his fifth birthday. For weeks, he had thought that the linoleum was one of his birthday presents. He thought of it as *his* linoleum. All the little things like that I knew about Philip, things no one else knew. Did he even consider that side of himself – the funny, off-center side?

'So,' he said. 'We should set a date.'

'You mean it?'

'Yes, of course I mean it.'

'Well…'

'How about February. We can even get married on Valentine's Day if you want.'

'Are you doing this because you thought I was implicitly threatening you? Because I wasn't.'

'I'm doing this because it makes sense. It's the logical next step.'

There was a steely look in his eye. I hoped I wouldn't regret pushing for the marriage vow. Would I want that vow so much if I felt truly loved? I didn't know. If Philip loved me more, perhaps I would want to marry him less.

'So it's settled,' he said, and squeezed my hand.

The waiter came with the dessert menu. Philip let go of my hand. The waiter said with a slight scowl, 'The creme brulee is very good tonight. It comes by itself or garnished with fresh strawberries. We also have blueberries in champagne sauce, and a chocolate mint mousse.' I wondered what secret heartbreak or hope he was hiding. I wondered who he went home to. Philip and I both ordered the creme brulee.

'Before the weather turns cold,' said Philip, 'we should go visit my Aunt Lavinia and Uncle Stuart.' His aunt and uncle lived at a family house on the Eastern Shore. It was called Azalea Grove and Philip had spent several childhood summers there. I imagined what it would be like to have a house with a name in the family. What would you call my father's house if you had to name it – Brick Box? Crabgrass Lawn?

Philip was immediately passionate when we got back to his place, but guilt made me clumsy. And the strangeness, the unpredictability of Harry, made my lovemaking with Philip seem more scripted than I'd ever noticed. After a while, however, Philip's sheer enthusiasm caught me up. There was a look he got towards the end, intent and compelling, that never failed to carry me along with him. The contrast between his bedroom and his outside self was exciting. His nakedness seemed more naked than other men's, his passion so much more astonishing.

I didn't want to let myself go. Somehow tonight it seemed too easy a solution, my body a traitor that led me into strange and thorny places.

But: 'Don't fight it,' Philip said in the soft voice he used to use when he first loved me and our lovemaking was still all discovery, and once he'd said that I couldn't.

*   *   *   *

At four a.m. I woke up starving. As I sat at Philip's kitchen table gnawing on a chicken leg, I thought about calling my family and announcing my news. Annette and Francesca would be relieved, Cynthia would be disgusted, and my father would tell me he expected us to have a priest perform the ceremony.

As for Philip's parents, they would offer us tepid congratulations and worry silently about what sort of plebeian brawl would erupt at our wedding. But they would be more contented than not. It was time for Philip to be part of a couple. Everyone in their world was coupled after a certain age. Even the gay people they knew had been together for years and years. Everyone in pairs, on this cozy Noah's ark kept afloat by old money and tradition.

I would now be one half of one of those married couples I used to envy when I went out for the paper on Sunday mornings, those married couples walking hand in hand down the street, their wedding rings shining in the sun. I would start to say 'we' instead of 'I', and to tell single women they didn't know how good they had it. Safe harbor, that was what I'd achieved. I would never have to hail my own taxi after a dinner party again.

Thinking about never being alone again is comforting at four in the morning, when your spouse-to-be is sleeping the sleep of the just, when you miss another man so badly you can't finish your fried chicken, when it feels as if the whole world is in on a secret you don't know.

Chapter VII

'Crisscross,' said Robert Walker to Farley Granger. 'Crisscross.'

Robert Walker's insanity was frightening precisely because he was so eerily mildmannered. Someone you'd never notice in a crowd.

The American Film Institute is drafty and utilitarian. There are no popcorn stands, no rowdy teenagers. I was wearing the thinnest of summer dresses, a twenties-style printed gauze with a long rope of cobalt-blue glass beads. I wanted to curl up in the circle of Harry's arm.

'You cold?' he whispered.

'No,' I lied.

I hadn't yet gotten around to telling him about my engagement. The ordeal with my family had been bad enough. They always rained on my parade, but in this case it was an absolute downpour.

'I'm happy for you,' Francesca had said, 'but I hope you realize that Dad won't go if it's not in church.'

'That will be his choice, Francesca.'

'Don't you think you're making too big a deal of this? Having a priest will make him happy.'

'My wedding isn't about making him happy.'

'Put it off for as long as you can,' said Cynthia. 'That way, I can have more time to talk you out of it.'

Dom and Joey had grunted their congratulations. Emotional events reduced Joey to a preverbal state, although he often waxed eloquent on a fuel injection blockage or the right way to spackle a bathroom. Even Dom, who could describe the plight of the Florida alligator so movingly that you forgot it was a predatory beast and wanted to send it checks, was illiterate in moments of affection. 'Good work, Di,' was all he said. Joey mentioned that now that I'd be a married woman, I should think about junking my '63 Dodge Dart and getting a solid, reliable used Cavalier he was fixing up at the garage – as if marriage promoted me to some grownup status I had hitherto lacked. Apparently it was fine for the single to go about on foot or in rattly old vehicles, like pilgrims, but marriage meant setting up in style.

My father had inquired if Philip would sign an agreement to raise the children Catholic.

Thus was this significant milestone in my life marked by my nearest and dearest. What had I expected?

Philip had said he wanted us to go together to the jewelry store and pick out a diamond. I'd never owned a diamond in my life. I'd just as soon have had the money to spend on my shop, although I couldn't tell Philip that. Just-engaged women wore rocks on their fingers – it was a primitive custom that couldn't be flouted. But I had always preferred sapphires and couldn't tell a good diamond from a piece of broken glass.

I had dreaded my evening with Harry, all the awkwardness of being with someone you'd slept with but didn't intend to sleep with again. But the second I saw him waiting for me under the Kennedy Center portico, I wanted to walk up to him as if I were entitled to put my arm through his, ask how his day was, count on all the familiarities that are the rights of legitimate affection. When he came towards me smiling his crooked smile, I felt like a nervous stranger – a stranger on a train.

We were both rapt as soon as the movie started. Harry didn't try to whisper in my ear or hold my hand. It was as though he had forgotten where he was. The way he looked reminded me of Cynthia that Saturday long ago when some kind neighbor had taken us along with her own children to see our first ballet, *Sleeping Beauty*. I'd been overawed and anxious, afraid I would do something wrong, but Cynthia had simply lost herself in the spectacle. Harry's absorption was the same.

We watched the credits while the theater emptied out.

'I feel like Chinese food,' said Harry. 'How about we go back to your neighborhood. You've got Chinese there, right?'

'There's the Yen Ching Palace. Right next door to my apartment.'

'Can we get take out and eat on your balcony?'

'I don't think that's a good idea, Harry.'

'What can happen on a balcony?'

'You're asking that after a Hitchcock movie?'

'I can be trusted absolutely when I have an egg roll in my mouth.'

In the car we talked about the movie.

'Did you know Robert Walker committed suicide not long after that movie was made?' said Harry.

'That's too sad. I wish I didn't know that.'

'But at least he made the movie first. When you think about it, everyone dies. Not everyone dies leaving something perfect behind them.'

The M.G. spluttered up Rock Creek parkway and onto Cathedral Road under the Taft Bridge. In summer Cathedral Road is a tunnel of green. The murky light made it seem we were driving under water. We had talked the movie over and had been quiet for a few minutes. Harry took my hand. When we got to my neighborhood he miraculously found a parking space in the alley behind my apartment. He kept holding my hand on the street.

'It's take-out, right?' he said before we went in the restaurant.

'Okay, but don't blame me,' I replied.

For Washingtonians who love Chinese food, the Yen Ching Palace is like the Shrine at Lourdes. The Yen Ching may not serve the *best* Chinese in the city (although I think it does), but that isn't the point. The point is the hostess with the penciled eyebrows and the great vintage wardrobe that features gorgeous brocade cocktail dresses from the 1950s. And the back table where, legend has it, Kennedy and Kruschev's emissaries settled the Cuban missile crisis. In the early days of detente with China, the diplomats gathered here to start patching things up. 'We serve more diplomats every day than the White House,' say the Yen Ching's matchbook covers, and unlike most matchbook cover copy, this is probably true. Yet it is also a place where a little old lady in support hose and a five-year-old winter coat could sit and enjoy a six-dollar moo shu chicken – and the staff would not only know her name, they'd know the name of her French poodle, which hip she'd had the surgery on, and which hair dresser did her hair at the Mona Lisa salon down the block.

There's a lot of advertising blather these days about restaurants and discount department stores and car repair shops that treat you like you're family. In my experience these places *do* unfortunately treat you like your family does – they ignore your opinions, expect more from you than you get back, and never have what you want when you walk in the door. The Yen Ching, on the other hand, treats you the way a family would in a perfect world: a warm welcome, a hot and savory meal, and compliments on how well you look or how hard you've been working.

We blinked in the darkness inside.

'This is incredible,' said Harry, who got the place immediately.

The bar gleamed with jewel-colored, dangerous-looking bottles. Near it stood a fish tank with miniature carp flashing gold and silver. Jade horses and carnelian vases crowded the shelves that ran the length of the big front room. There were peppermints for sale in a musty case by the door and off to the side, wooden phone booths with little seats and sliding doors, the kind they don't make anymore.

'The best thing about the Yen Ching,' I'd told Harry while we studied the take-out menu, 'is that you always know exactly what you're going to get. The General Tso's chicken is the same every time.'

'And that's a good thing?' said Harry, grinning.

'Just tell me what you want.'

'I want it all.'

When we got to my apartment I sat him out on the balcony. I kept a little folding table out there, and some ratty wicker chairs with ratty old pillows. Though the balcony looked more like a fire escape with its corrugated iron roof and iron railing, it was my own exclusive balcony and I liked to share it with select people.

Meanwhile, I bustled around my kitchen, hunting up forks and a bottle of white wine I'd kept on hand since June. The truth was, I didn't get much company. I met my friends at restaurants or coffee bars, and spent more time at Philip's place than he spent at mine. Frankly, my place made Philip nervous. It had none of the modern conveniences. Unlike Harry, Philip didn't enjoy the feeling of having stepped back in time. I might not either, if I'd grown up in the Victorian gloom of Montville, Alabama, and the Traynor family home, which appeared (from the photos Philip kept around) to be a Gothic manse that sucked up light.

We had hot and sour soup, spring rolls with mustard sauce, twice-cooked pork and pepper chicken. Over the balcony we could see the guys at the fire house lounging around. In the distance, the sky above Newark Street hill turned delicate shades of lilac, washed azure, and the palest mint green.

'You've seen *my* family,' I said to Harry after we'd finished our soup. 'What about yours? Are they still back in Queens?'

'My folks would never live anywhere else. But they aren't together. They're divorced.'

His father, whom Harry referred to as Big Jake, was a hopeless womanizer and an obgyn. One way or another, from what Harry said, this guy had his hand up a woman's skirt every hour of the day. Big Jake had left Harry's mother when Harry was five for the Sicilian widow who lived in the apartment one floor below.

'Do you remember much about your folks' breakup?'

'I remember my mother throwing a toaster at my father.'

'A toaster?'

'I know, I know. Why not a glass or something? She'd have had to unplug it first.'

'I saw this old Joan Crawford-Burt Lancaster movie where Burt Lancaster throws a typewriter at his wife. Of course, that was a manual typewriter. You wouldn't have to stop to unplug it.'

'I saw that movie too. I think we're the only two people in the Western world who've seen that movie.'

When Big Jake was unfaithful to the Sicilian widow in her turn, she did not take to Valium and crying jags as Harry's mother had. Sophia was made of sterner stuff. She called a few cousins who, whether or not they were really connected, threw such a scare into Big Jake that for years he never came to visit his son except in disguise.

'He'd wear these drugstore sunglasses and an overcoat. Even in summer,' said Harry. 'He would bump around because the sunglasses were so cheap he couldn't see out of them. We're talking about a man who was easily seventy

pounds overweight with a walrus moustache. Who did he
think he was fooling?'

Eventually Sophia remarried a plumber, and Jake was free
to come pick up his son in normal attire. But Harry and his
father never developed what you'd call a warm relationship.
From what I could tell, the father spent most of his time
regaling Harry with details of his exploits with women. There
was also the ongoing battle with the IRS. Big Jake owed them
thirty thousand in back taxes.

'Every Saturday he'd tell me, "I might not be able to come
for you next week. I might be in jail another time. But I love
you, that doesn't mean your old man doesn't love you",'
Harry remembered. 'This is a great view up here, by the way.'

No one would call my view a great view, but Harry made
me feel I had something private and particular to offer.

Harry's mother had been born believing that men owed
her, owed her big time, and Big Jake provided ample justifi-
cation for this assumption. For the entire year after Big Jake
left, she sat staring out the window. Once in a while she'd
open a can of tomato soup for Harry and his older sister.
Otherwise, they were left pretty much on their own. A week
after the divorce became final, Harry's mother took a vacation
to the Catskills, where she met Harry's stepfather, Sheldon.

Sheldon was an accountant. He made a good living, and
was looking for a wife to spend it on. Harry's pretty, fragile
mother was the perfect object for his pent-up tenderness and
his steady, affectionate ways.

'The only problem was,' Harry said, adding more pepper to
his pepper chicken from the side container of hot peppers the
Yen Ching always added to my order, 'The only problem
was, I don't think she was ever able to love anyone again after
my father. She blamed him for everything. After a while,
being angry at him became like fuel to her. She lived on it.'

Yet Sheldon and Harry's mother married, as people who

weren't really in love so often did back then. Well, even now, women like Harry's mother – helpless women who always look incipiently tearful – are never allowed to remain single for long. There was always some softy willing to take care of them. Whereas if you are feisty and efficient and know how to fix your own fuse when it blows, men run like jackrabbits.

Sheldon and Harry's mother settled into a life of quiet misery together. On Saturday afternoons, while Harry's mother napped (she was a gifted invalid, that was clear), Sheldon would take Harry to the Museum of Natural History, or to Barnes and Noble to browse through the archaeology section.

'Those were Sheldon's two big dreams,' said Harry. 'He wanted to be either a paleontologist or an archaeologist. He's allergic to dust, pollen, and every kind of insect bite, but he dreamed about digging up Troy. It was kind of touching.'

Harry's sister became a podiatrist, and Harry went to college and law school at Columbia. He had dinner with his father every six weeks, and saw his mother and Sheldon on holidays. When Harry and Nancy separated, his mother didn't speak to him for a month.

'She expected me to turn out like my father. She was always saying things like, "men are all alike, they'll always leave you in the end". I guess this proved to her she was right,' Harry said.

He'd stopped eating now, and was watching the firemen take down the flag. I wanted to stroke his hair and tell him to forget about all that. I wanted to run out and purchase his mother a gift membership in the Hemlock Society.

But all I said was, 'What about your father? What was his reaction?'

'Big Jake said I was better off single. He told me the older you get, the more women come after you. Once I asked him if he had any regrets about his own life, and you know what he said? He said he wished he'd played more golf. Honest, that's his one regret.'

'It's amazing they produced you,' I said, and even to myself my voice sounded ridiculously sappy. So I took the plates inside and began scraping them. Alone in the kitchen, I thought about how friendly I felt towards Harry, yet how that friendliness didn't seem to mute the desire I felt for him in any way. How strange. I'd always thought of those as mutually exclusive emotions.

When I came back outside, the heat had turned into that blissful August coolness that descends after sundown. Soon in the mornings I'd need a sweater as I walked to the shop.

'I like your neighborhood,' said Harry. 'It reminds me of Queens. My mother was always ashamed of living in Queens, but I liked it.'

'What's wrong with Queens?'

'It's the unclassy part of New York. I mean, even Brooklyn has a certain cachet, but Queens is just a big run-down old safe place to raise your kids. You know it doesn't even have its own postal code? You can't address a letter, Queens, New York.'

'We have places like that, only they're just names someone invented to put a Metro stop next to. Like Tenleytown. Queens is realer than that.'

'Yeah. I always liked it. I liked the leftover ruins where the World's Fair was in 1964. I liked this dingy Italian restaurant Sheldon used to take me to. But Nancy would never live anywhere but Manhattan.'

'You really like Cleveland Park? It's not the most exciting part of town.'

'But it's a place where you can sit on a front porch swing or take a long walk after dinner. It's a kind place. I like that.'

He had gotten to the heart of it there. In Cleveland Park,

cars waited for mothers with strollers to cross the street.
Shopkeepers called you by your first name. Even the schizo-
phrenic who lived under the bridge and displayed Magic
Marker signs about CIA assassination plots was afforded
kindness – his cup was full of dollar bills even when he was
raving.

My fortune cookie said, 'Prosperity lies ahead'. Harry's
said, 'A warm word is worth much.'

'Prosperity. That's a good one,' I had to laugh.

'You never know,' Harry said. We were sitting with our
feet up on the railing, drinking the last of the wine.

'Then remind me to buy a lottery ticket.'

'How did you get into this? The secondhand clothes business?' He said this curiously, not as Francesca would have
said it. Francesca's tone would have implied: a fine mess
you've gotten into.

'Well, I always loved clothes. Vintage clothes. Or designer
clothes I couldn't afford.'

'My wife believes that clothes oppress women,' Harry
remarked. 'She doesn't even own a pair of high heels.'

'Yeah, that's a real problem. Why worry about equal pay
and abortion rights when the Maybelline people are still in
business?'

'It's just a rule of hers never to be uncomfortable.'

'I don't trust people who have a lot of rules for their lives,'
I said coldly.

'She does have a lot of them,' he said. 'Hey. Her rules
aren't my rules, you know. Finish your story.'

I told him how I'd shopped at The Second Time Around
ever since I first moved to Cleveland Park eight years ago. I
got to know the woman who owned the place. Her name was
Mary Foley. Mary was in her sixties when I met her, a rail of
a woman with a scowly, disapproving face, the unfortunate
result of years of nearsightedness. She sold me my first Sonia

Rykiel sweater, a thin red-and-black-striped pullover. A buy
at thirty dollars.

Mary and I recognized each other in the way of people who
share a passionate interest. Mary never lied to me about what
looked good and what didn't. She never sold a customer an
unflattering garment. The clothes in her shop were carefully
drycleaned, and anything pressed or patchy she put in the dollar bin and gave the proceeds to charity. She chain-smoked
and dispensed advice, she took in consignments and gossip
from her regulars, and when people left they felt they'd been
on a surprisingly pleasant social call.

From Mary I learned the designers who suited me and
those who didn't. A 'yes' vote to Calvin Klein's clean elegance and flattering necklines; a 'no' to Emmanuel Ungarro's
cheerful prints and whimsical ruffles, adorable as they might
be. Like my mother, Mary loved the hidden beauties of good
workmanship that are too rare outside designer circles: a hem
properly finished with lace basting tape, a lovingly worked
buttonhole, a satin lining striped in old gold and rose. Fine
craftsmanship brought joy to her heart. When the new genius
Richard Tyler came on the scene, she pinned up magazine
photos of his line on her bulletin board with the words. '*This*
is good tailoring!' inked across the top of the page.

Many a skirt or jacket of mine got given to the Salvation
Army after it failed to pass the test of Mary's searing gaze.
Under her tutelage, I spent half what I used to on my
wardrobe, and looked twice as good. I was her apprentice.

One spring day Mary told me that she and her husband
were retiring and moving to Sedona, Arizona, as they'd
always planned. The shop would close unless she could find a
buyer. Two months later, my mother died and left Cynthia
and me a second insurance policy in the amount of thirty
thousand dollars, a policy no one in the family had known
about. She had left this money to us, she had written in a note

on the policy, because our other sisters had husbands to take
care of them.

When I heard this news, I shook myself out of a grief-
induced stupor, walked up Newark Street and asked Mary
what she'd accept for the shop's current inventory. She settled happily for ten thousand dollars. I quit my job the next
day, with five thousand in the remaining insurance money
and ten thousand in savings to live on. I took out a small
business loan later. Mary worked with me a few weeks,
teaching me how to do the books, how she sorted new
arrivals, paid consigners and priced the merchandise. Then
she wished me well and headed West. She wrote me a letter every two months on drugstore stationery with blue-
birds on it. I loved to see that bluebird stationery in my
mailbox.

'And here you are,' said Harry.

'Here I am.'

'Don't give up yet,' said Harry. 'I'm getting the feeling you
can count on one hand the people in this town who are actually doing work they enjoy.'

'Do you love your work?'

'I became a lawyer because that's what men in my family
do. We become lawyers, or doctors, or accountants. But the
funny thing is, it turns out I like it.'

Harry handled a grab bag of cases from criminal defense to
patent filings to probate challenges. He spent his days track-
ing down witnesses, sweet-talking prosecutors, and typing his
own letters, since his firm could afford only one-quarter of a
secretary for him. Sometimes he'd even serve his own sub-
poenas.

I thought, Harry and Philip are both lawyers, but a visitor
from outer space would never guess it, watching what they
did all day.

'Most of it's small-time stuff,' Harry said. 'But I'm not at a desk the whole time, that's the main thing. You have goose-bumps on your arm.'

'I'm always cold.'

'Let me help with the dishes.'

We stood at the sink side by side. I washed and Harry rinsed. Our elbows bumped.

'There's a cloth over there,' I said to Harry when we were done. But instead of drying his hands, he put his arms around me. When I turned and put mine around his neck, soap suds ran onto his collar.

We were holding each other so tightly I had to stand on tip-toe to avoid losing my balance. He murmured in my ear while he was kissing me, 'I'm sorry, I know I said I wouldn't do this. I thought I could handle a little temptation, but this is way beyond temptation.'

'It's okay,' I said.

'I can leave right now,' he told me while he pulled my dress down over my shoulders and trailed kisses across my collar-bone.

'In a little while,' I said, unbuttoning his pants, unbuttoning his shirt. He wore a sleeveless ribbed undershirt, just like the men in my own family did.

This time I noticed more. I noticed that Harry seemed to want me very much. When I went to put on a little music, he stared at me so hard that I just chose the first thing that came to hand, a Bach duet for harpsichords. His blue eyes glowed.

Is this because it's been awhile? I wanted to ask him, but it didn't matter anyway. Harry made love as if we were in a ramshackle bomb shelter with only an hour until Armageddon. He was irresistible and everything he did to me felt very, very good. It was as if somewhere, without knowing it, I had been building up a huge fund of grace and a benefi-cient goddess had decided to hand it over to me in one fell swoop.

After he was asleep – there was no question that he'd stay this time – I turned on the lamp and gloated over him. He never let go of me, even in his deep sleep. His eyelashes were black against his cheeks like a young child's, but his grip was the grip of a man who knows only too well that while you are sleeping, people may get up and leave you.

Chapter VIII

'About children,' Philip said. I was at his house helping him make dinner. He was a very methodical cook. I was usually assigned to chop celery and set the table. Tonight we were having shrimp with cilantro sauce. One of his father's secretaries had given him the recipe. All his father's female staff adored Philip. They'd all mothered him or fallen in love with him over the years. He had had affairs with two of them, Donna and Joyce. He was the crown prince.

'What about children, buddy?'

Buddy was an endearment I'd developed for Philip in our early days together, when I'd discovered he didn't like endearments. He winced at 'darling' or even 'hon', and I finally said, exasperated, 'What do you want me to call you – buddy?'

'Well, do you think you'll ever change your mind about having children?'

'I don't think so.'

'But you're just thirty-two.'

'There are natural mothers and then there are natural aunts, and I'm a natural aunt.' I said. 'It's like buyers and renters, stock speculators and mutual fund investors.'

'Don't make a joke about this,' in a tone that implied that he thought the alarm on my biological clock must be defective.

He was deveining shrimp while we talked. That's one of the drawbacks of settled love. Even your most tender and telling moments are hedged around with the mundane.

It was a week since I'd taken Cynthia's advice and closed the shop, a week and a day since that second night Harry stayed at my apartment. Since then I had spent one hectic afternoon in bed with him in his rented efficiency in Mount Pleasant, and worked feverishly with my sister every day, driving myself hard so I wouldn't think about my own duplicity. The guilt I felt about cheating on Philip was like a sharp, stabbing pain that came and went. It hit me especially hard at moments like these, when we were making dinner as we had hundreds of times before, the moments when one partner is taking for granted the security of the routine while the other – the nefarious one – is thinking that if I were with Harry we might be eating ribs from Hogs on the Hill, without all this time-wasting preparation. Philip didn't like barbecue or any traditionally southern food. As a child he had been forced to attend too many fundraising catfish fries.

I'd said to Harry, 'Philip thinks we're officially engaged.'

'What do you think?'

'I'm not sure. I would have been sure if it weren't for you. Now nothing makes sense.' There was a hollow just under Harry's shoulder where my head fit perfectly. Harry was stroking my hair and listening to what had gone wrong between Philip and me.

'February is a long way away,' was all he said when I finished, because after that I had kissed him and we'd made love again.

I loved going to bed with Harry. I thought about it constantly, whenever I wasn't thinking about my shop. My guilt towards Philip grew in proportion, but that didn't stop me from betraying him. For as virtuous and remorseful as I could be away from Philip, the second I saw Harry the idea of not making love to him seemed ridiculous. With Philip, I had to earn every tender word, every kiss and caress. Harry couldn't help liking and wanting me, and he didn't eke out his affection or schedule his passion for appropriate times.

I also cherished a measure of resentment against Philip for not expressing any interest in the renovations at the shop. He never asked about the shop, as if it were a private hobby of mine like his uncle's stamps or Big Jake's erotica. But then he'd always set himself against anything Cynthia had a hand in.

Cynthia and I had painted the walls a pale terracotta shade that the paint swatch called sunwarmed peach. We went to estate sales and thrift shops and found four brass standing lamps. We bought cheap wall mirrors from Murphy's five-and-dime for inside the dressing rooms. Cynthia knotted tulle around the corners of these, or pasted reproduction Victorian wrapping paper on the borders, so they looked classy.

From my father's basement she salvaged five wrought-iron garden chairs, which we spray-painted glossy white, one for each cubicle – 'So people will have someplace to rest their purse and to sit when they reapply their lipstick after they get dressed,' said Cynthia. When asked for these chairs, my father had grunted, 'Hell, I'm not using them.' I hadn't wanted to take anything from him, but Cynthia told me not to be squeamish.

We even created a three-way mirror for the common area by buying panes of mirror glass at Hechingers and cementing them to a carved wooden screen we discovered sitting by the curb of one of the big limestone rowhouses on Ordway Street.

The owner of the shoe repair shop had been glad to give up his window in exchange for my keeping his cards in a basket up front – plus hefty discounts for his wife and three daughters.

We had our own little cards made up that said simply

'Cynthia's – for the kind of clothes you thought you couldn't get in Washington' with our number and address. We were working on a flyer to announce our reopening, to put in dry cleaners and hair salons, on windshield wipers throughout Northwest, and in every restaurant window in the neighborhood, where Cynthia's charm had not gone unfelt.

Tomorrow the bags – peach and white striped, with white cord handles – would arrive, along with stacks of tissue paper. Suddenly, it was just like a real store. The whole effort had cost me fifteen hundred precious dollars, a figure I couldn't think about without hyperventilating.

Maybe I went on about these changes a bit too long. On the other hand, hadn't I listened to Philip describe his office rivalries, his pitched battles on K Street, and how the Federal Reserve worked?

Now Philip said, 'I was just wondering if your mind was made up. Children-wise. Do we have to close the door on that, Diana?'

'Can't we just say we don't have any immediate plans to have kids?'

He was squeezing the limes while I chopped radishes. I hate radishes but Philip's mother always served them with her salads, so Philip put them in salads too. But his silence was more than just the silence of the absorbed cook, so I tried again.

'As far as you can be certain of anything in this life, I'm certain I don't want children,' I said.

'How can you *know* something like that?'

'Trust me,' I said.

All my life I'd believed that once a woman became a mother, nothing interesting would ever happen to her again. She would be relegated to the kitchen, with the other mothers, while the men talked about world events in the dining room. The whole business of being pregnant and going through

labor, of which I had been hearing elaborate descriptions
since I was barely out of diapers, turned my stomach. As if
my mother's stories of what she went through weren't
enough, lately I had fallen victim to the modern trend of being
asked by married friends to admire pictures, sometimes even
a film, of the entire delivery.

There is something wrong in any set-up in which the
woman is the only naked person while everyone else stood
around fully dressed, with even their faces covered. There
you are, with your legs spread out like a wishbone, grunting
or screaming away. I, a person who needs to down three
aspirin just to get through her annual Pap smear, do not have
the fortitude for the delivery room. Childbirth is perhaps a
holy experience, but like most holy experiences I prefer that it
happen to someone else.

Children. Once you had children you could no longer stride
freely down the street. You would turn into someone's
mother. You would actually start to care about such things as
reading methods and carseats. You would gain weight and
neglect to lose it. You would spend years of your life dealing
with someone else's shit and spit-up and whining. You'd
have to fret about their nutrition, their bowel movements,
their moods and sleep habits. I had already gone through that
with my mother during her worst drinking times. I never
wanted to be responsible for the physical care of another creature again as long as I lived. When Philip got a cold, I was
hard pressed even to warm some chicken soup for him.

I used to explain this reasoning to every man who asked
me. But announcing that you had no maternal feelings
seemed to be a direct kick to the groin, as if you were person-
ally rejecting their sperm. Once I caught on to this, I kept my
eye out for men who did not want the family life. I'd thought
Philip was one of those men. When I had asked him early in
our relationship about children, he'd shrugged and said,

'They'd be a lot of trouble, wouldn't they?' Now he was musing on parenthood. And they say *women* are biologically hotwired to reproduce!

'It's just something to think about,' said Philip. 'Have you ever considered talking to someone about it?'

'I've talked to lots of people about it.'

'I mean, someone professional.'

'Forgive me if I don't classify this as a mental problem.'

'Forget it.'

'Do you want children, Philip?'

'I said, forget it.'

The shrimp smelled wonderful, of lime and basil and a dash of cayenne pepper. Philip had been cooking for himself a long time. He liked food that tended to the Creole or French, smothered in sauces, simmered for hours.

His kitchen showed all the evidence of a domestic spirit. There were copper pots and strings of garlic hanging from the walls, and blue-and-white-striped earthenware bowls in stacks in the open cupboards. There were no dishes in the sink. He'd even washed the cooking pots before dinner began.

In the dining room, there was the same aura of settled graciousness. Philip's townhouse had been built in 1900, and it had high ceilings and varnished hardwood floors. The dining room was airy and elegant, painted pale Wedgewood green with ivory molding. We sat at the octagonal oak table that had been in Philip's family for five generations. That table had been in America longer than anyone I was related to. It was so solid that it took four people to move it, and so big we had to sit side by side or in splendid isolation.

I remembered, as I took out Philip's Waterford wine glasses, how safe I used to feel in this house. I remembered one night two years before, when the city had had one of those freak ice storms that can hit in January. Outside the trees were glittering, and now and then you heard the crack of one of the frozen branches crashing to the ground. But inside Philip and I drank mulled cider, built a fire in the wide stone fireplace, and went early to bed, where we made love and curled up together to listen to the hail pelt against his skylight.

That night, Philip had stroked the back of my neck and said, 'Your skin is so soft. I never met a woman with such soft skin,' and in his voice was that tone of awe and tenderness that means a man is on the way to falling in love with you. I had gone to sleep feeling so cherished, cherished by him and by the mellowed, secure history he came with.

How had I come from then to now, from feeling so cherished to wondering if I'd measure up? I still loved Philip, his graciousness, his gentleness, his bookishness, his standards. He was familiar to me. But you could fall in love with habit and custom and confuse them with warmth and affinity. I have always been a creature of habit. For example, I always order the same thing every time I go Pettito's – the fettucini carbonara, because it was good the first time. I wear midnight blue but not navy because once, years ago, someone told me midnight was better on me. Maybe I wanted to marry Philip because I had wanted to marry him for three years now?

When I finally opened my shop, I'd been brave enough to say to myself, *this* is what I really want. With men, I'd never said that. I'd always said, what can you offer, what must I settle for? I had never listened to the far-off keening of my own desires.

'Philip,' I said, before we'd even tasted our food, 'I want to ask you something.'

'Okay,' he said, then jumped up to get the salt.

'Philip.'

'Uh-huh.'

'What I wanted to ask you is, what are you doing with me?'

'What am I *doing* with you?'

'What do you see in me?'

His face said, Why do women always ask these questions?

'I can't categorize it, Diana.'

'Just try.'

He gave me a patient, tolerant look.

'Okay. Um, you're nice to me.'

'Go on.'

He sighed. 'You make me feel good. You're not demanding.'

'Demanding?'

'You know, some women are so demanding. You get home from work and all they can do is badger you. How did your day go? Did you think about me? How do you feel? As if their primary goal in life is to figure out every little feeling you've got.'

'But Philip, those qualities you just named, they all describe how I act towards *you*. What about me do you like? *My* own qualities.'

'Didn't I just tell you?'

A friend of mine had recently confided that she had finally mustered up the courage to ask her husband to tell her more often that he loved her, and why. Her husband had answered, 'I'm still here, aren't I?' Did that answer say everything, or nothing? Sometimes I felt that the smallest toddler was more equipped to unravel the mysteries of life than I was.

After dinner, we lay on the couch and read. Philip put on a recording of the Brandenburg concertos by some Norwegian prodigy I'd never heard of. It was a cool night, but we were both too lazy to get up and build a fire. He was reading an account of the collapse of the Soviet Union. I read *Sense and Sensibility*. Every now and then he'd lean over and kiss my hair. Every now and then I'd tuck the edge of the blanket around his foot.

I lay there lapped in comfort with a man who had decided that, on careful consideration, he would rather not live without me, and I thought of Harry. His pointed questions and his accurate perceptions. His stories of his family. I thought of how unbelievable it was that any woman could have ditched him for some pompous microbiologist. I thought of how when he had stroked me and put his mouth between my legs and entered me from above and below I'd come so many times that I thought I would die of pleasure. I thought of the noises I made that, remembered, it seemed someone else had made. Of the noises he'd made, calling my name in the sort of frenzy of satisfaction I never thought I would inspire.

None of these reflections stopped me from making love with Philip that night. It was good, unrushed, untroubled by guesswork. Like the motions of the Mass, that was what married love would be like. It counted on the deep reflexes of familiarity, shared experience, and a faith in what lasted beyond the ephemeral moment of physical connection. Oh God, was that ever enough? What if you were so shallow you wanted passion and mystery to continue? What if you were temperamentally restless? What if just when you'd won a long struggle for the person you wanted, some lawyer from Queens wearing a discount rack suit made you forget everything you had worked for for years?

Before he turned out the light, Philip said, 'You asked what I liked about you. You're a kind person. You keep me from freezing up.'

'You keep yourself from that, Philip.'

'But you remind me of why it matters.'

Chapter IX

Harry and I were driving to the river on a chilly October Sunday. Philip was at home, racking up billable hours. He had been doing that a lot lately. He had also been nagging me about when I was going to start the process known as 'wedding planning'. Now, I know there are women who actually enjoy spending a year before their nuptials booking a reception hall, finding a church to (suddenly) belong to, planning how the pale apricot of the bridesmaids' dress will tone with the ribbons looped around the pews reserved for family, and generally reveling in every detail of The Big Day. But, as with nearly every feminine ritual I'd ever encountered, I was proving myself woefully deficient in the girlish glee and painstaking energy required to pull the whole thing off.

Mrs. Traynor, who had never spoken or even looked directly at me before, was suddenly calling up to inquire about the number of my bridesmaids and whether I had considered a candlelight ceremony. I didn't think I could tell her that my idea of the perfect wedding was running off to a justice of the peace before any of your family caught on, then throwing a huge rowdy party with no gifts allowed. Sneak away and do it without thinking too hard about what you're getting into – that would have been my preference. It was this sort of sourpuss attitude that had gotten me kicked out of Brownies.

Since there was no hope of a businesslike elopement
(Philip's first comment when I brought it up was 'It'll break
my mother's heart') I'd told Philip I wanted a quiet ceremony
with only our immediate families and our ten closest friends,
perhaps in one of the side chapels at the Washington
Cathedral – I was pretty sure Senator Traynor's pull could
extend to snagging a side chapel. Then dinner someplace
small and intimate, say the back room at the Old Angler's Inn,
and a quick getaway. But all the time I was voicing these pref-
erences, it felt as imaginary and remote as a game called
'Mystery Date' we'd played as children. In 'Mystery Date'
you opened a little cardboard door and there was a card
depicting your Mystery Date – a handsome doctor, a suave
businessman, or a nerdy Jerry Lewis lookalike. Mystery Date
was no more like real dating than the lists and deadlines I
scratched on a legal pad with Philip were like truly getting
married (although my tendency to draw the Jerry Lewis escort
had turned out to be predictive of my dating years). It was all
a game, a game I didn't like to think about too much. April
(we had decided on April, it seemed) was very far away. In
the meantime, there was Harry, and here we were driving in
his car on our way to the river and that was all that mattered.
All that mattered was what we were doing that afternoon, and
then looking forward to the next time I'd see him and the time
after that. It was terrifying how simple it was with us.

Harry was singing along to 'Me and My Bobby McGee' in
his offkey baritone. He took music seriously. He didn't just
listen to it, he absorbed it, and when he liked someone's
music he had to own it all. His tastes ranged from Gregorian
Chant to acid rock. His great hero was Pete Townsend, and he
had a number of violent hatreds, including anything written
by the Beatles after 1968.

Knowing this helped explain a bulky little package that had
arrived in the mail a few days before. It was a Tom Waits tape

called 'Rain Dogs', wrapped in a note written on plain blue airmail paper:

Dear Diana,

This tape is cued on Side 2 to the original version of 'Downtown Train' so that you can hear for yourself how much that no-talent, pseudo-sex-symbol, parrot-headed ripoff artist freak Rod 'I Suck' Stewart screwed it up while still managing to make money off the creative energies of others.

As for the rest of the tape, I'm sure it's not your style. So why am I sending it to you? I don't know. I think to really appreciate this music, you have to listen to it in a room brightened only by a flashing neon light filtering in from the outside through dingy Venetian blinds. (The sign is shouting something like, 'Girls, Girls, Girls, 25-cent peep booths' or 'Clean rooms by the hour. Sheets extra.') The air has to be filled with smoke from unfiltered Camels or Lucky Strikes, and your head has to be addled with two days worth of Jim Beam (no ice) and sixteen-ounce longneck Schlitz (no glass). As you strum your fingers on the bar, you have to glance nervously over your shoulder from time to time, checking to see if you're about to be pummelled by a jealous husband or the guy with the scar and the skeleton tattoo that you still owe big time from last week's visit to the pool hall on Heartattack and Vine.

But if you venture beyond the selected track, I recommend 'Big Black Mariah', 'Rain Dogs', 'Gun Street Girl', and 'Blind Love'.

Yours,
Harry

* * *

I had listened to this tape over and over. Now we were driving out to Glen Echo and Harry played 'Tommy' in the car. He tried to explain to me what 'Tommy' was about, but I was distracted by watching how he looked when he talked. That was all right, too, because Harry wasn't demanding some reaction or instructing me in that way men do. He was just talking about something he loved.

'So is "Tommy" sort of about the hopelessness that followed the Vietnam War?' I asked him.

'You don't even remember Vietnam, do you. Only people who don't remember it at all say, the Vietnam War, in that formal way.'

'I had a POW bracelet. And I remember the airlift on TV. You're only three years older than I am.'

'It's a big three years.'

'You're right. What are we even doing together?'

'You know what,' he said.

We walked by the river. The day was glowing and serene. The Potomac was slate-blue. The trees caught the last of the sun and burned like brush fire. We could smell woodsmoke in the air. Except for a few bicyclists and hardy walkers, we had the towpath to ourselves.

Harry's hair was growing longer. His wife must have liked it short. Now the curls were slightly shaggy, a better frame for the big nose with the bump in it where Big Jake had accidentally dropped him as a baby. He wore an old blue pullover that made his eyes the same color as the river.

'Do you ever hear from Nancy these days?' I asked as we rounded the bend past the lock.

'Yeah. Once in a while.'

'What does she say?'

'Nothing much.'

In sleep Harry wanted contact, proximity. He knew if I turned over, withdrew my hand from his, got up in the night.

He didn't wake up, but he would cleave back to my side as soon as I came back to bed. In daylight, he would hold my hand or pull me onto his lap. He had lived a long time with someone whose teeth were set on edge by his every emotional gesture, and it had made him hungry for affection and astonished by it. Once he said, 'Every time we make love, it gets better and better,' and the wonder in his voice told me more than he had ever said about his sex life with Nancy.

'Why did you marry her, do you think?' I asked now. I was asking him more and more questions, slipping them in when I thought he wouldn't notice.

'Oh, I don't know.'

'What do you mean, you don't know? You didn't wake up out of an amnesiac trance one day and find yourself married, did you?' (This had actually happened to Brice Covington.)

'I guess because she didn't especially want to marry me at first. She was a challenge. I met her at this dinner party. She'd just broken up with someone, this guy who wrote financial columns for the Wall Street Journal. She seemed so sad and lonely. She was very thin and frail-looking.'

'And how soon did you cheer her up?'

'We dated for a long time before she slept with me. It was a big deal for her. She was so bruised from her last relationship.'

'Bruised' must have been Nancy's word. A great sex-stalling word.

'The old boyfriend, he was a big deal. He appeared on those Sunday morning financial talk shows to predict what the interest rate would do. You know the type. He left her for a twenty-one-year-old student in one of his journalism classes.'

Bicylists cycled past us. An elderly couple holding hands smiled on us. A breeze blew off the river.

'Are you sure you want to hear this?' said Harry.

Was I sure? I wanted to hear about how his first baby tooth

fell out. I wanted to know about the first girl he kissed and if he'd ever ice-skated at Rockefeller Center and what five books he would choose to bring with him if he were stranded on a desert island.

After months of being wooed and consoled, Nancy finally consented to sleep with him. On their first night together, she left her beloved's arms to go floss her teeth. She never liked to make love more than once in a night. How horrible she sounded! How horrible the ex-wife always is!

I could picture Nancy so clearly. She would have medium-brown hair that she wore in some practical way when she was at the lab – in a low ponytail, or pulled away from her face with a simple tortoiseshell barrette. She'd have the sort of straightforward, sensible good looks that caused other women to refer to her a 'a terrific person' (something they never said about Cynthia, for example). Nancy probably wore sneakers with her business suit when riding to work on the subway, a despicable habit. Someday she would do groundbreaking research that would give her an eternal footnote in the med-ical books and help thousands of people she would never meet. But I wouldn't want to be stuck in an elevator with her; she'd probably pull out an improving book or use the time to write out her grocery list.

And yet, I realized, Harry must have married her for a rea-son. Perhaps it was that small cool distance between them. The idea of having to win this prize every day. Being kept on his toes. Nancy sounded like one of those pale, composed woman who always slightly despise the men they're married to. And Harry had been trained by his mother to believe that maintaining a marriage is more hard work than pleasure – that marriage is an act of will. He would have seen it through with Nancy. Men. Their boneheaded stamina was so touching.

Harry drew me off the path and kissed me. We walked down to the edge of the river where the trees hid us from view. There were no fishermen on the opposite bank. The only sound was the lap of the river and the crickets fiddling. Harry put his hand under my sweater. Then he pulled my sweater up and kissed my breasts. The air was cold and his mouth was warm.

'I've been thinking about mountain voles,' he said, stroking and kissing my breast.

'Mountain voles?' I asked faintly. He kept stroking.

'I met this neurobiologist a long time ago who told me that mountain voles are these little weasel-like animals who illustrate a baffling principle about the nature of attraction,' Harry said calmly. He put his arm around me. With one hand he continued touching my left breast, fingering my nipple. His other hand moved between my legs.

'You see,' he said, 'Prairie voles are very faithful. They spend their lives with one female vole and they get jealous every time another male prairie vole goes near her. But the mountain voles are sluts. They'll do it with anyone.'

'What's your point?' I whispered.

'This one biologist, he wondered, what made the difference? What made the prairie vole so faithful and true and the mountain vole such a heartless philanderer?'

He was kissing my neck. I put my hand under his sweater. I tried to reach down his pants but he held me away.

'This biologist found out that the brain of the prairie vole secretes this chemical during sex called oxytocin. Every time this prairie vole makes love to his wife, there's a big spike of oxytocin. And after they have that experience with a female vole, they associate her with it ever after. They're bonded together by this chemical euphoria. That's how I feel with you.'

The hand that had been on the outside of my jeans was sneaking inside them now.

'The mountain vole, he doesn't secrete much oxytocin

when he fools around. So he's always searching, searching, playing the field.'

'Envying the prairie vole,' I gasped, 'with his prairie vole stationwagon and its vole hole in the suburbs.'

My hand was finally on him. My hand moved up and down. I felt him grow.

'What about the foothill voles?' I said.

'I don't think there are any foothill voles,' said Harry. 'But it's so like you to ask.' He kissed me. His tongue stroked the roof of my mouth in a way that made me entirely open to him.

'There's no one around,' he said. 'Let me come inside you.'

Nancy would have said no, I thought. In a minute my jeans were around my knees. His hand stroked. I lay there, still as the day around us, drunk with lust, the whole warm earth at my back.

'No?' he said, and took his hand away.

'Yes.'

The sun was setting by the time we were back in the city. We went to dinner at a dark Italian restaurant in Adams Morgan, the kind with checkered tablecloths and parmesan in a shaker and wine-bottle candles dripping wax. Then we returned to my place and finished what we started, because the time on the river bank was nowhere near enough. I was beginning to be afraid I would never get sick of Harry.

It was only later, as I was slipping into sleep, that it occurred to me that he never really did explain, in his own words, why he married Nancy. Or what it was that she'd written to him lately.

Chapter X

The store was still closed in late October, still being transformed by Cynthia's inspirations and our combined elbow grease. We had made more racks by hanging wooden poles from the ceiling on bronze chandelier chains. Nothing said thrift shop, Cynthia said, as much as overcrowded racks. Cynthia had negotiated a volume discount from my drycleaner's and was vigilant about their work. A bunched-up shoulder pad or a damaged mother-of-pearl button and she was off to reproach them. On the windowsills she had put ceramic jars of lavendar, so the whole place smelled of spring.

For my part, I was calling Mary's old list of consigners, reminding them that I was ready and willing to take any of last year's unwanted purchases off their hands. I even offered to pick up the clothes myself, something no other consignment shop in the city did. With one call in five I would hit pay dirt, and the bundles and boxes of inventory that we brought in felt like birthday presents. Together Cynthia and I stripped and refinished a glass-fronted cabinet that had been languishing in Mary's storeroom. We used it to display silk scarves, gloves, handbags and belts.

I was reluctant when Philip suggested we should take advantage of my free Saturdays to visit his Aunt Lavinia and Uncle Stuart down on the Chesapeake Bay. Maybe it was because I felt like a fraud, making this pre-wedding visit when I was cheating on my fiance. And maybe it was that the shop had caught us up, Cynthia and me. We were experiencing the elation that is the reward of painstaking, affectionate toil. We worked together with the absorption we had once brought to our arcane childhood games. I didn't want to lose a whole weekend, but I didn't want the showdown with Philip that refusing to go would bring on. So it was settled that we would visit the last weekend of the month.

The only experience I had of the shore were the day trips to the beach my family took when I was a child. We could never afford to stay overnight, but somehow I remembered those days as if they'd lasted forever. My father, who would have been an excellent addition to the Donner Party, would pack the trunk of our old Buick with blankets, fried chicken, meatballs in glass jars, long sliced loaves of Italian bread, a jar each of olives and hot peppers, sugar doughnuts, and lemonade – gallons and gallons of lemonade he made himself, very lemony and very sweet. We'd get underway at five-thirty in the morning, Francesca in the front seat between my parents because she claimed she got car sick, the rest of us squeezed like anchovies in the back seat.

When we got there, my father would blow up our battered inflatable raft and my mother would settle under the boardwalk. She always had the same bathing suit, a black 1950s style even the nuns would have approved of, with a built-in bra and lining. It must have been hideously uncomfortable, but my mother believed being ladylike meant making certain sacrifices. She rarely left the shade of the boardwalk, fearing the sun's effect on her white skin. Meanwhile we were in the water with my father, who had taught us all to be daring swimmers. He was a good teacher, my father. During those days at the beach, he turned back into the big rollicking kid he must have been before too many children and not enough money made an angry, bitter man of him.

We'd swim out, far beyond the point where our feet could touch the bottom, and ride the swells of the waves just before they broke, two of us on an inner tube my father had bought for fifty cents at the junkyard, two of us on a styrofoam board we'd found abandoned on the beach. My father was the flagship of the fleet with small Joey beside him on the raft. We'd stay out until we were blue with cold, then come in and eat fried chicken from the tin cooler in the trunk. On the way home, my father and mother would sing together. They would sing, 'Tell Me Why', 'You Are My Sunshine', and 'The Big Rock Candy Mountain'. My mother had a wavery soprano; my father a true baritone. And though we were only gone a day, it seemed like weeks in the sun to us.

Life at Azalea Grove wasn't for day-trippers. Azalea Grove was a hundred-year-old clapboard belonging to Philip's aunt on his mother's side of the family, Aunt Lavinia Duncan, and her husband Stuart. They lived there from April to October. This branch of the family came from Arkansas, not Alabama, and was slightly less wealthy than the Traynors. But they, too, had been in America since the republic was first thought of.

Azalea Grove was on a rise overlooking the bay. Here the sand was yellowish, moist and crumbly, and the beach was littered with mussel shells, fragments of water-polished glass and the occasional shipwrecked crab. Behind the house was a stand of pine and a greenhouse where Philip's aunt spent most of her days. The greenhouse and vegetable garden were connected to the main house by herringbone walks. The place took its name not from any azelea bushes on the property, but from a great-great-grandmother named azalea who had died young. Now, in late October, only a few straggly yellow roses clung to the doorpost.

'You're not at all as I pictured you,' were the first words

Philip's aunt said to me. However, her manner was so gentle
and loquacious it was hard to take them as an insult. Uncle
Stuart simply shook my hand. I would learn that except when
he was playing Crazy Eights or out in his treasured motor
boat, he was generally silent.

Philip told them about our drive while I stood and looked
around me. The place was like the inside of a ship. From the
foyer I could see small cozy rooms with walls all of pine
wood and built-in shelves and cubbies in unexpected places. I
loved it at once, the warm glossy pine, the squat Victorian
sofas, the ripply round mirror in the hall, the conch shells
clustered on the mantelpiece.

We were put in separate rooms. I'd expected this, but it
still made me feel childish and illicit. In my bedroom were
an antique barometer, a high four-poster bed, and a wicker
rocking chair that Aunt Lavinia informed me she'd been
given as a girl and brought with her from Pine Bluff when
she married. I stayed there for longer than was polite,
unpacking my bag, feeling nervous, shy and greasy among
all these fair-haired and restrained people. Aunt Lavinia
was in her seventies, but she still had faded strawberry
blonde hair. Uncle Stuart's was silver. They were both
weathered and dignified as no old person in my family
was, and alike as two bookends.

I knew this weekend was bound to include some terrible
breach of manners on my part. Upperclass manners were still
all guesswork to me. I could usually manage to pick up the
right silverware, but the smaller points, such as choosing the
proper hostess gift, were puzzling. Philip had suggested potpourri, but potpourri was so grandmotherly. I really hated it,
and I hated to give what I wouldn't buy myself. In the end I
bought a fancy boxed whiskey cake from a gourmet shop up
the street from mine. Then I wondered if they'd be thinking,
'Oh yes, she's part Irish.'

When I emerged, Philip and his uncle were in the hall, talking in those low staccato monosyllables that pass for conversation among men. I went to the kitchen, thinking to offer to help his aunt. She didn't need any help, she said, so I stood there, not wanting to sit down while she wasn't, not wanting either to get in the way. Finally I leaned against the doorframe, casting about for topics. She asked me how I met Philip, and I told her.

'How did you meet your husband?' I asked her. She laughed an embarrassed laugh as she filled the tea kettle.

'I was teaching school,' she said. 'In Little Rock. I had a prize pupil, a girl I wanted to make sure went on to college. One day her family asked me for supper. I went, of course. She was such a bright girl. She was a lovely girl, too.'

'What did she look like?'

'Let me see, she had dark hair and pale skin like yours, but her eyes were blue. So there at supper was her oldest brother. He didn't say much at dinner, but he offered to drive me home.'

'Love at first sight?'

'Well, actually, I didn't like him much at first. I thought he was fresh. And he was three years younger than I was. But I let him drive me home. And he grew on me.'

'How long have you been married?'

'Thirty-five years.'

Philip and his uncle were out in the hall, examining some flies his uncle had tied the day before.

'What happened to his sister? Did she go to college?'

'I'm afraid not. Her family just felt there was no reason. This was nineteen fifty-eight, you know. She got married to a very nice fellow. An accountant. But they were killed in a car accident in nineteen sixty-one.'

'I'm so sorry.'

There was a silence while she moved around, gathering

cups and sugar, getting a tiny Alice-blue ceramic pitcher of milk from the icebox.

'What were you wearing the night you met your husband?' I asked.

'What was I wearing?'

I knew Philip was listening, or imagined he was. There was a slight wince he gave sometimes, when I did something not done in his world, a reaction so unconscious he wouldn't have admitted to it. He left off examining flies and came into the kitchen.

'Not everyone remembers her whole life by what she was wearing, Diana,' he said.

He was smiling, but I could see I'd put my foot in it. I was always getting tangled in a web of invisible do-not's with Philip's family. But why shouldn't she remember? Philip's aunt must have been very attractive once, in an elegant way. Now her face was a network of wrinkles, the kind of wrinkles made by long exposure to sun and salt air. She was a sparrow of a woman, with fragile bird bones that I could have broken with one hand. But the line of her jaw and cheekbones, her continued slimness, told me she must once have been a pretty girl. Surely she'd have had a little vanity, enough to remember a favorite outfit, a sentimentally significant outfit.

'I can't say,' she said. 'A skirt and blouse of some kind, I'm guessing.'

We all drank tea at the pine table in the kitchen. The tea was weak, and the milk curdled a little in the cup. The sugar was lumpy with damp. Philip and his Uncle Stuart discussed stock market fluctuations. Aunt Lavinia told Philip that Mrs. Strickland down the road had died. It was expected. Cancer.

In my family, such an announcement would have provoked rapid inquiries. How had the deceased acted in her last days? Had she had much pain, preferably a dramatic sort of pain? What did she look like in her coffin? What sort of spectacle had been made by her relatives at the funeral? We still enjoyed remembering how my Aunt Lucia, who had killed my uncle Franky with her nagging, had thrown herself sobbing across his casket at the wake. This was quite an achievement for a woman of two hundred pounds who was four-ten in her stocking feet. She'd had to do a little jump, like a Pomeranian leaping for a biscuit, just to launch herself across the corpse.

But here no one asked these interesting and necessary questions. No one raised a voice. It was so quiet you could hear the drone of a bumblebee in one of the late roses. After lunch, which consisted of slices of ham on dry storebrought bread, Philip's uncle invited us out on the motor boat.

'I thought we would show her the pilgrim cross,' he said. 'Where the Ark and the Dove landed.'

Although he referred to me in the third person, I had the feeling he liked me, in a mild way. He didn't seem nonplussed by me, as his wife was.

Philip followed me to the door of my room.

'I can't believe you asked her that,' he said.

'I'm sorry.'

'You didn't do anything wrong. It's just that it's the last thing she would remember.'

'Could you do one thing for me, Philip? Could you not grade my behavior while I'm here?'

'Don't you think you're being a little oversensitive?'

'Humor me then,' I said, and closed the door on him. I pulled on a thin smoky-blue sweater that came down to my knees over black cotton pedalpushers, and changed into black sneakers. When I emerged from my room I could see from Philip's face that he disapproved of this outfit. The outdoorsy girls he had brought here before had probably worn Chinos and Fair Isle sweaters.

The boat made me a little seasick. I clung to the built-in

seat, hoping I wouldn't disgrace myself with nausea. It had
been cloudy while we drove down from the city, but now the
sun came out and dazzled right through my sunglasses. The
water was a little choppy. Uncle Stuart looked supremely
happy.

When we reached the pilgrim cross, a huge stone cross on
a point overlooking the water, I felt better. Philip's uncle told
me that it was here that the Ark and the Dove, the ships of the
English Catholics who settled in Maryland, landed after
months at sea. They had held their first Mass on this spot
where the huge stone cross now stood. The cross had been
erected sometime in the 1930s, Uncle Stuart said.

'They must have been deliriously grateful to get off that
ship.'

'Yes. Originally they meant to go to Massachusetts, but
they got lost. Being Catholic, of course saying Mass was the
first thing they did.'

'Wouldn't you want to murder someone after being cooped
up for months like that?'

'I'm sure it's happened,' said Philip's uncle. 'Look at that
woman,   Dorothy   Bradford,   who   disappeared
off the Mayflower. They said she must have thrown herself
off the side, but there's nothing to prove she wasn't pushed.
Who would know?'

'That's right,' I said. 'She was depressed, someone sneaks
up behind her, and presto, her husband can get a new wife for
the New World. All that time at sea, the pressures of an
unhappy marriage might tip the balance toward homicide.'

'You'd certainly be homesick for dry land,' Philip's aunt
put in, uncomfortable with the dark turn the conversation was
taking. I had the feeling that if you could get Uncle Stuart to
himself, the conversation could take several interesting dark
turns. I liked people like that, people with secret passageway
and subterranean rooms in their psyches.

We ambled around the point for a while. The feeling of the place was holy in the way of places where great human feeling was once expended, like certain Civil War battlefields that the tourists haven't spoiled yet. Philip didn't hold my hand or touch me at all. I'd have liked some gesture of solidarity, but then his aunt and uncle didn't touch each other either. It was impossible to picture them making love, so separate, so dried-up they seemed.

The sun was dropping over the water as we motored back. Philip's uncle let me steer. Once a fugitive smile crossed his face. If only it had been just his uncle, not his aunt, I had to get to like me.

Dinner was more ham, served with potato salad from a plastic container and some iceberg lettuce. Dessert was canned peaches, Aunt Lavinia saying she would save the whiskey cake for a special occasion. I knew they were old and probably didn't care much about food, but they had lots and lots of money. Did they live like this always? Did they never splurge on a steak? Over dinner, Aunt Lavinia described some plant clippings she was shipping to Philip's mother. The plight of the Chesapeake Bay crabbers was discussed.

I could see that to Philip this was normal. Normal food to be served by a relative, normal conversation among family. Normal old people.

In my family, old people didn't dry up like this. Being old was a license to act as outrageously as you pleased. Our old people complained at length about their digestive tracts, outdid each other in reciting embarrassing stories, ate and drank copiously, made groaning noises when they got up and sat down, and asked you pushy and interfering questions. Philip's aunt and uncle did none of this. They might have been waxworks for all the emotion they displayed.

After dinner we played Crazy Eights and Twenty-One. I fell into a mild trance of boredom, having been taught the

game and achieved a basic competence. We played for nick-
els, and Philip and Uncle Stuart were quite competitive. At
the end, Philip winning best two out of three, his uncle grew
somber and went off to bed.

'You could have let him win,' I whispered to Philip.

'He wouldn't have let *me* win.'

That night, in the high creaky old bed, I was kept awake by
doubt and anxiety. Here in this timeworn house that spoke of
the importance of the marriage bond and the family over the
renegade individual, I felt like a sham. When I was with
Philip, I lived the life of rightness and propriety. When I was
with Philip, I could pretend I was like other people in
Washington, people with stock portfolios and family reunions
and vacation homes and serious careers. When I was with
Philip, Harry became a madness in my eyes, I cudgeled
myself with guilt. But when I was with Harry, the whole
world seemed to right itself. What I had to say seemed interesting and witty, and what I wanted, whatever I wanted,
seemed perfectly natural, whether that was some specific act
of love or cannoli for breakfast.

Had any other woman who had slept in this bed shared
these thoughts, the thoughts of an adulteress in the making? I
tossed and turned, as a two-timer deserved, and when I finally
fell asleep I dreamed of my grandfather. In the dream, he was
rocking me in Aunt Lavinia's wicker chair and singing an old
Italian hymn to St. Nicholas, his patron saint. His comforting
smell, of earth and sweat and the chicory he liked to pick from
the side of the road, was all around me.

I woke up feeling horribly homesick. I lay there and
thought of my grandfather, whom I thought of briefly every
day but hadn't really remembered in years. All my baby pictures were with my grandfather. There was only one of me
with my mother, taken the day of my baptism. In this photo, I
am wearing the long lace dress she bought at Lord and

Taylor's when Francesca was born. I lie on my grandmother's cabbage rose couch that my mother always hated. The dress is three times as long as I am. My mother is arranging a fold of the dress, as if I were a doll on a satin pillow, and she is looking at the fabric, not at me. I'm just a little black-haired speck with a monkey's face, lost in billows of white lace.

My mother was laid up for several weeks after my birth, which explained her big-eyed, frail appearance. I'd been a Caesarean, having managed to wind my umbilical cord around my neck. While my mother recovered, I was given to the care of my grandfather, which I never really left. Failing eyesight had forced him to stop driving his knife-sharpening truck, which stood in the driveway and was regarded as an eyesore by the neighbors. He needed work to do, and I was at hand.

My grandfather fed me and fed me, as a guard against delicacy. He never gave me baby food, but instead he carefully prepared mushed-up meatballs, chopped escarole in chicken broth, and biscotti soaked in the milky sweet coffee he liked to drink. Under this treatment, I quickly became a very fat baby. In pictures I am bouncing on my grandfather's arm, my chubby white legs against his gnarled forearms, one baby hand plump on his face, about to snatch at his glasses. We are both laughing hugely, the tough old paisan and his fat little granddaughter with the bright red cheeks.

Like Uncle Stuart, he liked his card games, especially a game called Scopa that he and Cynthia used to play. They would both cheat incessantly and then yell accusations at each other. Like Philip. Cynthia didn't believe in the condescension of letting people win.

I grew into a skinny tomboy and my grandfather grew, so slowly I can't remember it happening, into a senile old man. He died while I was away in my first year at college. By then I had become just one more person who cared for

him, who emptied his bedpans and brought him his coffee,
who reassured him when he cried anxiously, who grew
impatient with his endless questions and demands. I can
remember the day he died, standing in the middle of the
academic quadrangle in the April sunshine, unable to cry. I
was wearing a pink blouse and a flowered skirt. The blouse
didn't fit right at the neck, and that feeling of ill-fitting, of
the bunchy tight collar. I always connect to that day he
died. I felt more relief than anything else, relief that the
burden of caring for him had been lifted from the family
still at home, relief that I would no longer have to empty
bedpans or cut his cornsilk hair. To have the death of
someone you love bring relief is a terrible thing, it is
worse than sorrow itself.

It was too hard to think of my grandfather in this place so
far from the places he'd been used to. The only way my
grandfather would ever have encountered people like Philip's
aunt and uncle was if he'd come to their back door to ask if
they wanted him to sharpen their knives and fix their broken
lawnmowers. To stop sad thoughts of him I played the alphabet game: name a category and find an example starting with
every letter of the alphabet. Tonight it was flowers. Aster,
begonia, carnation, daffodil. Then, for some reason, I began
to miss Harry. Miss him terribly, that empty-stomach missing
for which there is no comfort. When he'd heard I was going
away for the weekend, he had grown very quiet.

'Do you not want me to go, Harry?'

'It's not my call.'

'I'm asking.'

'I want you to do whatever you want to do.'

This wasn't the answer I'd hoped for. Would he ever say he
wanted me to leave Philip? Ever show jealousy? I had. I'd
asked him what Nancy had written and he'd said. 'Just stuff
about how bad she feels about the way she treated me.' This

answer sent a chill up my spine. It did not sound like Nancy to apologize unless there was something in it for her.

I wanted to pry, but he distracted me. Harry knew a million ways to distract. We were always eating, walking, or fooling around. Harry rediscovered for me the city I thought I knew. He took me inside the Historical Society building, a Gilded Age extravaganza, and got the docent to give us our own private tour. He dragged me to the Georgetown flea market on a Sunday afternoon. He showed up at my door with tickets to *Henry IV* at the new Shakespeare theater. We held hands on the couch in the lobby of the Shoreham and watched political celebrities walk by.

Lying in the family bed at Azalea Grove, I wanted Harry so badly I thought my desire would fly along the highway to him and wake him up in his rented, scruffy bachelor apartment. I would have cried into my pillow, only Aunt Lavinia would be sure to notice waterstains on the pillowcase.

In the morning there was a walk along the beach and lunch at a beat-up old crab house that overlooked a tidal creek. The tables were covered in paper for those who wanted to hammer at crab and lobster with little wooden mallets. A ship's wheel with a spoke missing hung over the bar. The waitress asked Aunt Lavinia when they were returning to town. The owner, a plump rosy Mr. Fezziwig, brought us our drinks on the house.

During lunch, Uncle Stuart discovered my father had been in the war and grew almost talkative about U.S. military strategy in the Pacific. I felt I'd finally achieved a credential, and was meanly delighted to see the conversation taken away from Aunt Lavinia for all of twenty minutes.

On the way back to Washington, Philip held my hand, which he rarely does when driving. I had passed muster.

'That wasn't so bad, was it?'

Yes, I should have said, I stayed a stranger the whole time. And no matter how beautiful your family's world is – the sunset over the bay, the weathered wood and burnished history of that house – it isn't a world I will ever have any title to. But one kind word can always silence me, so I said it had been wonderful to get out of town for a few days, and that his relatives were very nice people.

Chapter XI

Francesca and I were having lunch at a lousy Greek restaurant across from her office. The reason for this lunch was that Cynthia's had to have a Christmas mailer, and Cynthia and I had decided it was time for something that actually showed the clothes. That was where Francesca came in.

We were eating gyros. The onion taste would stay in my mouth all day, no matter how much I brushed my teeth. Who would eat Greek food when they could have Italian? But Francesca thought it was exotic. The place was in a basement and the plastic tablecloth was sticky. Francesca was too cheap to go to any restaurant with real napkins.

Cynthia was back at the shop, waiting to say I told you so when Francesca turned us down. Cynthia's had reopened to little fanfare, but we didn't let it discourage us, and business had picked up. Some days now we had as many as twenty customers, thanks to word of mouth, and our flyers and business cards.

'We're selling accessories now,' I told Francesca, leading up to the favor.

'What kind of accessories?'

'Hats and jewelry.'

'Who'd buy a secondhand hat?'

'They're not secondhand.'

Through a shop in Georgetown, Cynthia had discovered a

woman named Rafaella who made straw hats decorated with dried flowers. On the hatband of the hat she wrote in silver ink simply 'Rafaella.' The shop hadn't wanted to share its source. They reckoned without Cynthia's years of experience in wringing fees owed her for modeling and small-budget films from shifty low-rent business owners and budding directors. Cynthia could track down anybody.

'Rafaella?' said Francesca. 'What kind of name is that?'

'Her real name is Marcy. She changed it because she felt she wasn't a Marcy and it was ruining her life to have a name that didn't express her personality. That's what she said, anyway.'

'No one is anything they started out as anymore,' Francesca complained. 'You don't like your big hips, you get surgery. You don't like your name, you change it. You feel like a woman in a man's body, no problem, just go from John to Joanna.'

Francesca, however, was exactly what she started out as. A good Catholic girl with a good Catholic girl family and good Catholic girl job. Working as a medical assistant was almost the same as being a nurse. My father, for example, understood Francesca's job, or thought he did. He probably thought she sat at a wooden desk in a nurse's cap, making appointments and handing out lollipops to children who'd been good for their shots.

'She's willing to do twenty hats on consignment,' I said. 'They're so pretty, if a customer doesn't wear the hats, she can still buy one to hang on the wall.'

They were lovely hats, straw boaters with clusters of dried iris and baby's breath and white and peach roses. Rafaella had provided some serious fall hats, too – a black felt broadbrim with a floppy black velvet bow, claret and navy berets with antique jewelry pinned to the front, little fawn and cream cloches with a silk pansy appliqued over the right ear. When I met her, I could see she was only honoring common sense in changing her name. She had delicate, pen-and-ink features and a cloud of curly golden hair and looked nothing like a Marcy.

'When I get married to Simon,' Cynthia had said when the hats came in, 'all the bridesmaids are going to wear Rafaella's hats.'

'Have you heard from him then?' She and Simon had had three more fights on the telephone, and now they were officially not speaking. Meanwhile her visit dragged on, while she terrorized me with new ideas and bullied me into a slow-growing success. One day I had said, 'I don't know where the shop would be without you, Cynthia. I don't know where I'd be,' and she said, 'Oh, you'd have figured things out.' We both knew I wouldn't have.

'Surnami did a reading for me over the phone. He said this was a temporary period of chaos and separation, but the final outcome would be that I will marry this man. That's exactly what he said.'

'If someone's a psychic, why do they need a phone line? Can't he just channel into your aura or something?'

'Don't be so cynical, Diana.'

Simon's wife Delia had moved in with him again for four days. Then she'd moved out. She confided that for the past year she had been having an affair with one of his best friends on the show, the guy who played likeable doctor Tom Sinclair. Dr. Sinclair used to have a great storyline when his wife Sylvia was being stalked by an escaped mental patient, but now his appearances were limited to breaking it to people that they were going to die and looking dubious about whether or not major characters would emerge from comas. Cynthia and I had watched *Covington Heights* the day before. Dr. Tom was telling Brice Covington his suspicions that Mrs. Moultrie's death was not from natural causes.

'But I thought her heart was bad,' said Brice. 'I thought she could go at any time.'

'These symptoms,' said Dr. Tom, then left a long dramatic pause, 'aren't entirely consistent with heart attack. I can't sign this death certificate. I'm asking for an autopsy.'

'Come on, man,' said Brice. 'Your imagination is running away with you.'

The camera cut to Olivia/Charmaine eavesdropping outside the door of Brice's study, her eyes narrowing.

'Did you see how tense Simon was around Pete?' said Cynthia. 'Did you see how broadly he played that scene? That's not like him at all.'

'It's exactly like him. The guy can't order a sandwich without hamming it up.'

'He wrote me a beautiful letter,' said Cynthia. 'He said he was working to make space for me in his life.'

'Christ. Why don't you go out with Mark Romano?'

Mark Romano had been to school with us. He ran his own restaurant in Bethesda, The Tuscany Table. The Post had called it 'a sprightly twist on Northern Italian'. He had blond hair and intense bright blue eyes, he played ragtime piano in his spare time, and he worshipped Cynthia.

'I did. I even slept with him. But it's all just a distraction.'

'How nice for Mark.'

'Mark knows the rules.'

Now I told Francesca, 'Cynthia also found a jewelry designer who makes necklaces of silver wire woven around bits of beach glass and antique china fragments. Not really my style, but they'll sell. They fit that wood nymph look that's in fashion this fall.'

'I never know what's in fashion,' said Francesca, with the air of someone who was above such things. This meant she felt insecure.

'That's because you have a timeless, classic style,' I reassured her.

We were a complete contrast today, as always. She was wearing a charcoal-gray cashmere cardigan, pearl earrings, and a heavy pleated gray skirt – basically an update of the uniform that had looked so good on her in high school. I was wearing a dark red twill shirt-jacket from the fifties. The shoulders were squared off but not overpadded and the waist was lovingly fitted. There was two tiny v-shaped pockets on the chest which helped me appear a tiny bit bustier than I was. With the jacket I wore black wool cigarette pants. I also wore a filigree stickpin, a cameo on a black velvet ribbon Cynthia had given me, and one of Rafaella's bracelets made of antique cufflinks. My hair was curled all over my head; Francesca's was smooth and held back in her usual grosgrain headband. She wore no makeup, only a little Chapstick. I wore blood-red lipstick and ivory powder.

'Cynthia told me about your window display,' said Francesca.

'It was like making a diorama. Remember the dioramas you used to make for Sister Mary Isadore's social studies class? You did one of a frontier stockade with cotton balls for cannon smoke and a little well with foil for drinking water.'

'No, I don't remember that,' said Francesca.

Our window display was set up like a stateroom on the Queen Mary, with a steamer trunk and a cluttered dressing table full of art deco silver lipstick cases and powder compacts. Cynthia had even found an old sea-green velvet powder box filled with the original powder. A price sticker saying twenty-five cents was still on it. Over the mirror were draped three bias-cut chiffon dresses from Donna Karan, who was born knowing more about making women look good than any male designer could ever learn.

Francesca said, 'So what was it you didn't ask me on the phone?'

'Well, we're doing a Christmas mailer. It's going to be a six-by-nine card with metallic gold ink saying Happy Holidays from Cynthia's. And one side will be photos of women wearing the clothes from the shop. Cynthia really thinks it's time we showed some of the actual clothes, and I agree with her.'

'So who's going to model?'

'Well, Cynthia of course ... and then, we thought, you.'

Francesca didn't say anything. I rushed on.

'We could take the pictures in local places people will recognize, like Dumbarton Oaks and White's Ferry and the porch of the National Gallery of American Art. And in front of the carousel at Glen Echo. Cynthia's friend Paul will shoot them for free. He owes her a favor.'

'Don't be ridiculous,' Francesca said. 'I'm not a model.'

'Look, Francesca, it would be such a big help to me. You don't have to be a professional. In fact, a superglamorous look would more likely alienate Washington customers.'

'Cynthia's the model.'

'You're a completely different type from Cynthia, but you're also beautiful.'

'Oh right. Why don't *you* model?'

'It looks too egotistical having the owner of the shop model. Besides, I squint when the flashbulb goes off and then I get those red dots in my eyes. You looked just like Natalie Wood the night of Dad's party, Francesca. You take a gorgeous photograph.'

She squirmed in her chair. Francesca discouraged compliments. She did this because she'd had a lifetime of having her looks disparaged by my mother. When she was fifteen my mother had told Francesca that while she was attractive she would never be beautiful, so she should make the most of herself. My mother thought of this as helpful and honest advice. Francesca had cried in her room for an afternoon, and after that had never once asked my mother's counsel on any item of clothing, any shade of lipstick. Jerry had bought her a diamond eternity ring for their fifteenth anniversary, but I had never heard him call her beautiful either. He was a practical man who believed love was a matter of deeds, not words – that if you were faithful to a woman you never had to tell her you liked her dress. As for me, I'd learned a long time ago that Francesca would bite my head off if I so much as admired a pair of her shoes.

'You know, Francesca, did it ever occur to you that Mom wasn't the most reliable person when it came to telling you how you looked? Did it ever occur to you that she might have been jealous at just how beautiful you are? It was Mom who was attractive but not beautiful. Not you.'

'That was a long time ago,' said Francesca. 'I forgot all about it.'

It would have been heresy in Francesca's eyes to blame my mother, a dead person up in heaven with the angels, for anything. So many things were heresy to my sister. I could never say to her, 'I am having an affair with a not-yet-divorced man while also sleeping with my Presbyterian boyfriend. Whichever one I wind up with, I do not intend to have children or a Catholic wedding.' Francesca had become the Church's representative in our generation. There's one in every large Catholic family – the one who owns a little bottle of Lourdes water, never forgets a Holy Day of Obligation, and prays for the return of siblings who have lost the way. The good one, who in earlier times would have been destined for the convent. What an excellent nun Francesca would have made. I could see her as an abbess with an iron grip.

'Think of this as a favor, Franny.' I hadn't called her Franny in years. 'Didn't I come to Dad's party? Didn't I keep my mouth shut when he gave those gloves I bought him to the Infant Martyrs clothing drive?'

'How did you find out about that?'

'Cynthia told me.'

I'd gotten to her. She's always felt guilty about her most-favored-nation status with our father.

'Won't you just help me out this once? Paul will make the whole thing so easy.'

'He's some guy Cynthia's carrying on with?'

'No, he's gay. He's just a friend of hers from all those years ago when she did *The Rainmaker* at that playhouse in Bethesda.'

'Jerry won't like it.'

'Jerry won't mind a bit.'

'This was Cynthia's idea, wasn't it.'

'No, mine. Francesca, my shop is in trouble. You're my sister. Are you going to help me or not?'

She cut the rest of her gyro into tiny, square pieces. The waitress, a comfortable-looking woman in a corduroy skirt and tight black t-shirt, came by to see how our lunch was.

'Delicious,' said Francesca with a big smile. 'You can bring the check whenever it's convenient.' All of us Campanellas can turn sickeningly polite at the drop of a hat. We all have those slightly formal, endearingly deferential public manners of lower-class children raised among upper-class children.

'You don't have to make up your mind until you see the pictures, Francesca. We won't use them if you hate them.'

She put down her napkin.

'Okay. But you'll be sorry.'

When we said goodbye in front of the medical building where she worked, I put my arm around her.

'Thank you. You won't regret it. We'll have fun.'

On the subway, however, try as I might, I couldn't think of

a single occasion Francesca and I had had fun together. Well, there was a first time for everything.

Unfortunately, this was not it. That Saturday we paid Rafaella to watch the shop and were ready to go by nine a.m. First we went out to Glen Echo, the old amusement park down by the river on the Maryland side. Paul started with a few easy shots, Cynthia and Francesca standing in front of the old fortuneteller's booth.

Francesca didn't exactly take direction like a pro. Every time Paul positioned her, she'd say, 'This looks really stupid, doesn't it. I look really stupid.' When Cynthia did her makeup, she'd complained that it was too heavy, even though we told her people made up more heavily for the camera. She was too cold, then too hot, though it was one of those beautiful Indian summer days. She was sure the hair spray would make her break out. She didn't like the herbed mayonnaise on the sandwiches I packed for lunch, she wanted diet cola not regular, and she needed to go to the bathroom every eight minutes. At Dumbarton Oaks, she was convinced she would be stung by a bee, even though it was far too late in the season.

Luckily, Paul turned out to be one of those soothing photographers who brings out the best in even the most stiff and uncooperative subject. He found a way to use Francesca's stiffness, to make it look like shyness and contemplation. He talked to her about the religious education program she headed at her parish, asking her questions about the wall-sized Advent calendar she was going to have the children make and the difficulties she had with the choir director.

'They obviously couldn't run the place without you,' Paul commented, and was rewarded with his subject's first spontaneous smile. Paul had a gentle, ascetic air that I could see had allowed Francesca to forget he was gay. He was wearing a white linen shirt with a mandarin collar and a brown woolen vest, and I knew she would refer to him as 'a sweetheart' after he left.

Near dusk, Francesca even agreed to take some final shots at the Rock Creek cemetery.

Rock Creek cemetery is the most Southern and romantic cemetery in the city. It sits on a wooded hill above the creek, and from the road it resembles a small Victorian city of the dead. We trudged up the side of the hill and waited while Paul sighted shots. The damp ground sent cold shivers up our legs.

'Just think of all the dead people under us,' said Cynthia. 'Think of their chilly fingers clutching our ankles. Like the end of that movie *Carrie*.'

'Be quiet,' hissed Francesca, as if the dead could hear us.

'You be quiet,' said Cynthia. In the car Francesca had made a disparaging comment about National Endowment for the Arts grants and 'people who think they have talent'. Cynthia had taken it as a slur on her acting career. I was far less afraid of the ghosts of those buried here than of open hostilities between my sisters.

Paul had gone over the hill, leaving me with his camera bag. In the fading light the marble of the tombstones and mausoleums seemed to glow from inside. You could hear the cold babble of the creek below. All around us were angels in stone. Slim, warrior-like angels chaperoning souls into heaven or protecting the tombs of the righteous. Drooping Edwardian angels, slim and despondent. Cherub and toddler angels guarding the graves of little children.

'Ready,' called Paul.

'I'm not moving another inch,' said Francesca. She stood there, immobile as a monument, regarding the epitaph of Marjorie Jane Howard, aged four, only child of loving parents Francis and Rebecca Howard.

In the end Paul had to come back down and take her picture right there.

'You're tired,' he said sympathetically. 'We pushed you too hard.' Whereupon the pugnaciousness left her face.

'You are so unprofessional,' said Cynthia to Francesca on the ride home.

'You're the professional,' said Francesca in insulting tones.

'That's because I've done tougher jobs than leading the parish Brownie troop or sucking up to Father Flynn.'

Only Paul's mediating presence kept the ensuring discussion from turning into the sort of fight they had had after my mother's funeral. Like my father and brothers, Cynthia and Francesca can hurl invective at each other one day and be sunny and companionable the next. Their anger is intense, but it never lasts long. I believe this may be why Italians have fewer heart attacks. How unfortunate that I took after the brooding, grudge-holding Irish side of the family.

When the contact sheets came back, none of the shots gave a hint of the many aggravations of that aggravating day. The graveside shot of Francesca was a serious and touching photograph, deliberately grainy. The late light drenched the scene. An inch from her shoulder was the chubby hand of the angel. Francesca's dark hair, her big dark eyes, the way her face and the angel emerged in light against the dark foliage and gray shadows, were haunting but not frightening. Momento mori. In the picture, one silk rose falls off her hat and onto the grave. None of us thought of arranging that, it simply happened.

I couldn't bring myself to use that picture in the mailer. It seemed so private, a side of my sister only the camera could call forth, or maybe just an illusion.

But there were so many other good shots that when the contact sheets came back I found myself circling frame after frame: Cynthia among the terraced roses at Dumbarton Oaks, in a minidress by Betsey Johnson. Both of them on the carousel at Glen Echo, riding on grinning horses that rose and fell in counterpoint. We chose forties-style suits by modern designers for that one, Francesca in cream crepe with black piping and Cynthia in gold, both wearing hose with a back seam, modern, strappy pumps and earrings made of chunks of crystal. Francesca sitting calmly on the up escalator at Dupont Circle in a black satin cocktail dress, the banks of steel stairs rising behind her like Jacob's ladder.

When I showed the proofs to Francesca, she said, 'These can't be me.' She looked at them for a long time, examining them through the loupe we'd borrowed from Paul.

'They're beautiful, Francesca.'

'I guess a good photographer can make anyone look good.'

How I wanted to hear her say one nice thing, one sentence with a whiff of agreement or enthusiasm. But after she left I began thinking, thinking about the scared sixteen-year-old in that cinderblock room at St. Agnes, wondering if her mother would ever let her back in the house. She had loved her baby enough to accept eviction. That was brave. It was brave to have her photo taken when she was so scared of that, too.

I had loved my mother, but how much easier that love had been made for me. My mother framed the paintings I made with the set of oils she'd given me for my eighth Christmas. My mother attended my college graduation nearly sober. My mother had told me I was pretty during those awful adolescent years when no boy would look at me. None of that had been offered to Francesca.

No wonder Francesca clung to the Church, for in return for living by its rules she had the assurance of being a very good girl – an assurance my mother had never given her. My mother, who had never breathed a word to Francesca about birth control, had blamed Francesca for getting pregnant. My mother, who was a lousy Catholic, had hidden behind Church dogma as an excuse to condemn her oldest daughter. My mother to her dying day criticized Francesca for 'not making the most of herself' while sewing prom dresses and cocktail dresses and bridesmaid gowns for her other three daughters, whispering in our ears about how irresistible we were. None of that for Francesca, no spare morsel of maternal tenderness.

I had a six-by-ten made of the Rock Creek cemetery picture and sent it to Francesca in an elaborate silver frame bordered in lilies, her favorite flower. My note said, 'Many thanks from a grateful sister.'

The next time I went to her house I looked for the photo. It wasn't in the living room, or in her little office, or Jerry's workout room. But when I went upstairs to use the bathroom, I spied it on the night table next to her bed, with my note tucked into the frame.

When I came back downstairs, Francesca said, 'You haven't called Dad in two weeks. Is it too much to ask you to pick up the phone once in a while?'

Then she told me she knew a priest who would marry Philip and me without making much of a fuss over my ambiguous status. Then we all sat down and ate tuna casserole with crumbled potato chips sprinkled on top. Francesca liked Middle American food like that, recipes torn out of some housewives' magazine, the sort of food she thought a regular mother would make.

Chapter XII

One thing about Washington: it's a town, not a city, and it has nothing of the wonderful anonymity that someone with a guilty secret could find in Los Angeles or Chicago. In those sprawling cities, you can slip out of your own life and into another just by leaving your neighborhood. But Washington doesn't have the sheer land mass to hide in, having been built on real estate grudgingly donated by Maryland. And its middle-class neighborhoods are crammed together in Northwest, cheek by jowl. Since nothing would have driven me to indulge my love for Harry in the outer suburbs at some Holiday Inn, I was taking a real chance running around Dupont Circle, Adams-Morgan, Cleveland Park, and Georgetown with Harry. I handled this risk by simply refusing to think about it, the way you'd push an overdue bill to the back of a bureau drawer if you were overdrawn.

But while the logistical implications were avoidable, the guilt was a houseguest that had come to stay for the duration. Later I realized that it was a measure of my love for Harry that I was willing to pay the price I did to see him. Many nights I'd wake up from a dream that I'd killed someone and was about to be arrested. I couldn't remember whom I'd killed, only that I'd done something that cut me off from the daylight world forever. Once I dreamed I was in charge of a gurgling infant whom I'd somehow left at the coatcheck stand at the National

Gallery. When I returned to claim the baby, I had lost my ticket and was told to leave the premises by a sternfaced librarian type. In the murder dream, Philip appeared just as the police van was taking me away, wearing the disappointed expression he assumed when I'd sad something tactless or wore an inappropriate outfit.

I knew what I was doing with Harry was wrong, and no rationalization applied to it. Yet at the same time, to eat and sleep and laugh with Harry felt so right in itself that no sense of sin was attached to it – as long as Harry was in the room. But let me as much as run to the kitchen for a glass of water and the guilt surged back, so that often I would stand alone in the middle of the kitchen floor, paralyzed with remorse, while Harry wondered what was taking me so long.

'Worry about that later,' said Cynthia when I suggested coming clean to Philip.

'What are you, Scarlett O'Hara?'

Indeed, when we were teenagers she'd once come to a costume party as Scarlett, dressed appropriately enough in a hoop skirt made of a pair of old green velveteen curtains from my mother's dining room (the hoop part was made from old coat hanger twisted into a circle and tied together with basting tape). She'd been a big hit in this outfit, whose neckline was a mere decorative edging around her award-winning breasts. I had gone as a gypsy, and everyone thought I was a flower child, a misapprehension that caused me to suffer the entire evening.)

'I should worry about it more,' I said.

'How can you tell Philip about Harry until you know this thing with Harry will last? Why cause him all that suffering?'

'Oh, so not telling him is a real kindness. I get it. You're such a Jesuit, Cynthia. And what about Harry? He never says anything but he hears me telling Philip I'm going home to put my feet up when I'm going out with him. He hears me lie.

That must make him think of Nancy. He's got to make the comparison.'

'For one thing, you aren't married to Philip. For another thing, you'd be surprised at the comparisons men don't make. They don't have our ability to relate one emotional situation to another emotional situation. They're kind of like dogs. No memory. Pretty immediate physical needs that overshadow everything else. You worry about the men in your life because you're afraid of discovering how simple men really are.'

Maybe she was right. It would break my heart, but maybe she was right. In Cynthia's view, inherited from my mother, women were farseeing and crafty, capable of masterly planning and fine nuances of feeling and expression. Men were brutes, in the old-fashioned sense of the word: clumsy and simple. In my mother's version, the battle of the sexes was like the Revolutionary War. Women were the cunning resourceful American guerrilla fighters and men were the stolid British in their target-red uniforms. Women hid in the trees and moved under cover of darkness. Men marched in straight lines and were easy to wound.

I longed to believe that some men were intricate, and that some women could risk the occasional forthrightness. I wanted to believe there were times of truce, that men and women could occasionally embrace across the barbed wire.

One night it happened, the close call I hadn't let myself think of. Harry and I had had a late dinner at The Dancing Crab, which is up by the former Sears building on an unfashionable little strop I thought Philip would never visit.

Harry loved The Dancing Crab, where you ordered your steamed crabs by the dozen or half-dozen and the tables were covered in brown paper. You were supplied with wooden mallets and tiny lethal knives. I was squeamish about using these instruments. I'd crack a leg open and leave the whole body alone. But Harry was a pro after only two visits, and he was fascinated by the place because he'd never been to a crab-house before. He liked to tie on the lobster bib I refused to wear, and go at it. And he liked his unhealthy meal as unhealthy as possible – with the crab meat dipped in butter, a basket of hush puppies, and a few beers to wash everything down.

'This place satisfies a primal urge,' he said after his fourth crab. 'Like a buffalo hunt.'

'It's not like you caught them yourself,' I snapped. I snapped only to hide my foolish delight in *his* foolish delight. Even as a baby, Philip had never looked this unaffectedly happy – I knew, I had been shown baby pictures by his aunt and uncle, at my own request. Philip had been a solemn, squinty-eyed child.

Harry was grinning. His bib was halfway round his neck. He dismantled all my share for me, since it pained him to see me wasting the best parts.

I must love him, I reflected, because I didn't even care that his hair was a mess or that his cuff had just landed in the butter. Every twenty minutes our waitress would come and top off Harry's beer from a plastic pitcher and refill my lemonade, smiling at us with the pitying smile experts bestow on rank amateurs. Harry had four beers. He was celebrating – one of his clients, accused of stealing a car, had had the charges against him dropped, mainly because Harry had done the leg-work of proving the kid had an alibi. While Harry's client was a noted graffiti artist whose work decorated warehouses along every subway stop on the Orange Line, he had never been in serious trouble before, and he was one scared teenager. His sweatshirt, his first name and his height happened to match the thief's, and the two friends who could corroborate his story that he was shooting hoops at the time of the theft both had prior records.

Harry had tracked down a teacher who placed his client on

a high school basketball court in Northeast ten minutes before
the car was stolen in Adams Morgan. Few other lawyers
would have taken the trouble – especially since in all likeli-
hood Harry would waive the fee. The kid's anxious parents,
working four jobs between them, made barely enough to
cover their mortgage.

When I listened to Harry talk about his cases, I realized
how much pro bono time he put in, how well he was coming
to know the dangerous neighborhoods like Shaw and Capitol
Heights. Sometimes he even went to interview witnesses at
Lorton. When I thought of my darling walking into one of the
toughest prisons in the country with his shit-eating grin, I
wanted to clutch his arm and beg him never to go out by himself again.

Harry pounded his wooden mallet on his tenth crab and
flagged the waitress down for more hush puppies. We were
talking about sitcoms of the 1970s. I pointed out that most of
them featured dysfunctional or non-nuclear families, reflecting a significant change in how the country perceived itself.
Harry said I was being academic.

'No, I'm not,' I said. 'You can't help noticing it.
Petticoat Junction – just those three beautiful girls and that
weird old uncle and the wholesome yet strangely ineffec-
tual aunt.'

'Bobby Jo was my favorite,' said Harry. 'You look a little
like her.'

He catapulted a hush puppy at me with his fork.

'Or take *Lost in Space*,' I said. 'With the obviously, *dis-
turbingly* pedophilic subtext between Mr. Smith and the kid
with the sticky-out ears. Why do you think that robot was saying. "Danger, Will Robinson" all the time?'

'That kid was so annoying he deserved to be the toy of an
entire chain gang,' said Harry. 'And the robot looked like a
Hoover vacuum cleaner. Talk about cheesy.'

'So name me one late sixties or seventies sitcom that had a normal family in it,' I said. 'Or even normal people.'

'Abnormal people are a staple of comedy. We're abnormal and we're pretty funny. You're ignoring the really important question of what were the words to *The Gilligan's Island* closing theme. Not the opening theme, but the closing theme.'

'Don't get in a theme song contest with me, buddy. You'll lose every time.'

My favorite theme was that beautiful ballad about Seattle from *Here Come the Brides*. Harry's was a catchy number from *It's About Time*, which a show that involved two astronauts stranded in the caveman era. We both thought *Green Acres* represented a peak of inspired lunacy that had only been equaled by the original *Bob Newhart Show*. We could talk about stuff like this for hours.

When we finished our stroll down memory lane, Harry tossed me the car keys. The night air was pungent with wood smoke and we dawdled towards the side street near Fort Reno where he'd left the M.G. Just as we were passing a tony Brazilian restaurant, its door opened and there, silhouetted against the golden rectangle of light, were Philip and his mother.

Sometimes I wonder if I'd have been spared any suffering if I'd been forced to confess to Philip then and there. If the streetlights had been just a little brighter, or Philip and Mrs. Senator Traynor were the sort of people who looked around the street more. As it was, I pulled Harry over into the doorway of a pet store.

He thought I was being affectionate, but when I hissed, 'Philip. With his mom,' his arm around me went still and heavy. They passed within five feet of us. Mrs. Traynor was wearing her blue wool coat *a la* Pat Nixon and dark blue pumps with gold buckles. She made a comment about the weather – something like, 'Chilly, isn't it?' and Philip agreed

that it was. Then they passed out of our range of vision, which
was obscured on one side by a window full of hamsters and
on the other by a pizza joint where we could see three teenage
employees sweeping floors and wiping the counters down for
the night to the accompaniment of jackhammer-loud heavy
metal.

'So that's him,' Harry said as we began walking to the car
again.

'That's him.'

'Dresses nice, doesn't he. Looks like a real bigshot. That tie
probably cost what this entire suit did.'

'It's what he has to wear for his job.'

'For his whole life, more like.'

'I'm sorry that happened.'

'Hey, you sleep with an engaged woman, you're bound to
let yourself in for these awkward moments. I knew the job
was dangerous when I took it.'

He had that blank look he gets when his feelings have been
hurt.

I said, 'Harry, maybe it's time I talked to Philip.'

'It's your decision. It's always been your decision.'

I wanted to promise him right there that I would break my
engagement. But he hadn't told me he loved me, and I was
waiting for those words as if for some magic permission.
Women will often dare anything on the strength of that con-
viction, but without it I was a regular Hamlet, weak-kneed
and quavery.

When we got to my place, I figured he'd say he didn't want
to come in, but instead he parked the car and we sat there, our
first uncomfortable silence pressing hard on us. Then he said,
'Life with you is complicated. This whole situation is complicated. But I'd rather have a complicated mess with you than a
smooth, easy ride with anyone else.'

In my living room, he folded me in his arms before he took

his overcoat off. All of a sudden I was five years old again,
back when my father, coming home from work on a cold winter night, would catch me up as he came in the front door and
hold me tight. I had forgotten that I used to run to meet my
father in the evenings. By the time I was ten or eleven he was
always returned home angry at the end of the day, and we
dreaded his arrival. For a long time I had forgotten that safety
and warmth and comfort was ever mine for the asking. Being
held by Harry brought it all back to me. Yet still I didn't have
the courage to ask him, 'Do you want anything more than
this?'

Chapter XIII

The article in the *Metro Dispatch* said. 'Vintage Gets a Hip New Twist', and it was all about Cynthia's. The lead read, 'Washington is a town where, more than in any other, it's possible to wear the wrong thing. And women's clothing establishments reflect that dreary fact. Now along comes a new entry that thumbs its nose at the rules. It's called Cynthia's, and you can't come out of there looking like June Cleaver no matter how hard you try.'

The *Dispatch* was a trendy little free newspaper, Washington's pale equivalent of *The Village Voice*. It ran long articles on Ward politics, chafed the mayor on his taste for cocaine, reviewed zydeco, punk, and alternative jazz bands, and supplemented its meager revenue by running ads other papers wouldn't accept – ads for wife-swapping groups, dominatrixes, and massage parlors. The *Dispatch* was as cool and hip as Washington got.

'Look at this,' I said to Philip, slipping him the torn-out page under the table. It wasn't very easy for him to look at it, since we were sitting in the semidarkness of a banquet room at the Washington Hyatt. We were there for the Hibernian Unity Foundation Peace Awards Banquet.

The peace awards were not a recent addition to the Foundation's yearly events. In a foundation like this one (which would be better titled, Friends and Relations of the

IRA) being a gunrunner didn't disqualify you from receiving
a peace award. Even the priests and nuns sprinkled liberally
throughout the audience were probably aiding and abetting
from the rectory basement and the convent storeroom. I was
sympathetic to the Irish cause and didn't blame them, only
myself for having agreed to come.

Philip had taken advantage of my euphoria over the article
to persuade me to accompany him. He had to come as a favor
to his father, who couldn't make it but respected the clout of
the Irish-American lobby. A lot of these Irish senators had
influence on health care issues, so as a good insurance industry lobbyist, ex-Senator Traynor couldn't afford to ignore
them.

I'd read the piece to Philip on the phone but I wanted him
to see it himself. He said, 'That's great. That's just great,
Diana, I mean it,' folded it and put it in his pocket. Then he
went on talking with the woman to his left, a horsy woman
with one of those shellacked bobs political women all have.

The horse-woman was saying, 'Well, he used to be at
Commerce, but you know what it's like there these days.
Then he went over to Interior, but there was that old feud with
Jay Strabotski, so he only stayed there a year. Last I heard he
was consulting out of his home.'

All around us was the din of celebrating Hibernians. I had
never seen so many silver-haired men with red faces. There
was a bottle of whiskey in the center of every table, intended,
our program informed us, for a door prize. Many of the tables
had decided not to wait.

Only our table was immune to conviviality. Because
Philip's father had bought it, it was full of insurance lobbyists
and pharmaceutical kingpins. A full table at the Hibernian
banquet – that was what the insurance lobby would want to be
remembered for next time the notorious senator from
Massachusetts or the illustrious senator from New York

Second Time Around 151

started talking about the need for Congress to pass a law forcing insurance companies to continue to provide insurance even when their policyholders actually got sick. Our table alone was absorbed in shop talk. Ex-Senator Traynor hovered over it like a serene Presbyterian ghost.

The women wore boxy plaid suits and matronly dresses with patent leather pumps. I looked shamelessly provocative in a curvy two-piece by Nicole Miller, a dress that would have been considered quietly sexy in New York or L.A. As usual, I was the only dark-haired person at our table, aside from the waiter. Even if you weren't in a business full of WASPs (and I was sure a *few* Italians and Armenians must be involved in running the insurance industry), you always hired Barbie-and-Ken types to do your lobbying.

I had not made a hit with this group. They had looked me over and dismissed me as without influence. My clothes gave me away. Unless your idea of dinner dress was garb appropriate for a distant relative's funeral, you couldn't be mistaken for someone who worked on the Hill. This being obvious, the men simply ignored me. Here, being pretty, charming, or intelligent didn't count if a woman couldn't remember who had been George McGovern's running mate.

I grabbed Phillip's arm while the mandarin orange salad with almonds was being taken away.

'Did you see what it said? It said, "These sisters are the kind of odd couple who more often than not find success." It said we were "a law unto ourselves in the dowdy code of Washington fashion."'

'Congratulations.'

He didn't look happy.

'What's wrong with it?'

'Nothing's wrong with it.'

'Then act like you mean it when you congratulate me.'

'Okay, the only thing is, did they have to refer to Cynthia

as "an icon of sexuality"? Did they have to put in all that about her being a *Purrr* centerfold and the *RosePetal* girl?'

'That's part of what makes us newsworthy. You know that. Besides, the *Dispatch* runs those Rosepetal's ads.'

'I don't call that newsworthy.'

'This is great publicity, Philip. *Free* publicity. We couldn't have done better if we'd written it ourselves.'

'Well then, I'm happy for you.'

But he didn't look happy. His cleancut features had a pinched, contracted look. Harry never looked that way. When he was angry he scowled, then we fought, then we were done with it. When Philip was angry I was treated to broken dates, days of conversation about the weather, and this tight-lipped averted face.

Dinner was a tough unidentified cut of beef, underdone carrots, watery cabbage, and of course, soda bread. I tried to talk to the man on my right. He told me why health care reform would be a disaster for American business.

I said, 'Don't lots of small businessmen go without health insurance because they can't afford it?' and he said, 'It's more complicated than that,' and turned to the woman on his other side. As often happened to me at these dinners, I was reduced to playing with my food and thinking how I'd like to be home.

Philip, however, was enjoying himself. His look of dignified annoyance had vanished, replaced by a delicate pink flush that spread to the roots of his golden hair. He and his equine neighbor were talking about a recent poll which had revealed that, when it comes to winning the public's trust, insurance companies fell below used car salesmen, politicians, and third-world dictators.

'Of course, you can manipulate polling data any way you want to. We're just an easy target,' said the woman. She was wearing a lime green scarf printed with little boxes and

secured with a big gold pin in the shape of a turtle. I would
have dressed in flour sacks before lime green or anything in
the shape of a turtle touched my body.

'Aren't you even happy for me a little?' I said in Philip's
ear.

'Of course I am,' he said, 'I just don't know why your sister has to be so notorious.'

I shut up, as I always did. Cynthia's career, after all, was so
politically incorrect, so much what I would never have done.
But then something new happened. I shut up but my brain
kept talking. It said, who are these people? Who is Philip,
born to the purple, to carp at my sister who made a living
using the face and body God gave her, sheer chutzpah, and a
hell of a lot of hard work? What did he know about the trade-
offs real people had to make to get by? Harry knew. Just yesterday Harry had said to me, 'I feel like a coward running
away to Washington. I feel like a coward because I couldn't
stick it out in New York with Nancy still there.' Harry lived
in the same world I did, a world where your self-respect got
tarnished and your family often made you feel like a worth-
less person, and you paid a small, real price for every little
thing you got.

Just yesterday, too, Harry had stayed late at the shop, helping me move shelves and stack boxes. Just yesterday, we had
gone back to my place and made love, and eaten the kind of
makeshift dinner people eat when they are too passionate to
plan meals – scrambled eggs with diced ham and melted
cheese on stale Italian bread. Harry had asked me, 'If Philip is
so great, what are you doing with me?' And I had wanted to
say, I thought it would wear off, this thing with you, but it
doesn't wear off, it only gets stronger and stronger. But
instead I answered, 'I don't know.'

A strange remote feeling washed over me, as if I were
about to faint. I was so apart from these people that any

minute I expected to leave my body and retire in astral form
to the kitchen to fraternize with the waiters.

A wiry nun (in plainclothes, since even Irish nuns didn't
wear habits anymore) rose to the podium to introduce a priest
to be honored among the other peacemakers that evening. The
priest in question had attracted several influential American
investors to a brewery that was giving productive jobs to former thugs. Now that peace had broken out in Northern
Ireland, the brewery had bright prospects. The man on my
other side gazed at the good Father with a polite, attentive air
that meant he was thinking of something else altogether, perhaps actuarial tables.

Tears came to my eyes. What was I doing here, wasting one
of the glorious evenings of my rapidly dwindling youth
among people who couldn't even admit it when they were
bored, next to a man who was ashamed of my family, who
had proposed to me more out of inertia than inclination? My
wrongs flooded back to me. Senator Traynor still treated me
more like a former constituent than a prospective daughter-in-
law. Philip ignored me for women who didn't pluck their eyebrows, women who knew what the Trilateral Commission did
all day. I couldn't live like the good Catholic girl I'd been
brought up to be, but I couldn't seem to find another way to
live that fit my skin, either. No matter whose banner I shel-
tered under, I would never belong. There were only two
places in the world where I felt exactly right: in my shop and
in bed with Harry.

Any minute the tears would overflow and run inky black
down my face – for unlike the other women at the table, I was
wearing mascara. To have emotions at all, that was the sin.
Philip would never love me as I wanted to be loved. He would
always reserve a small, disapproving part of his heart for crit-
icizing me. Never, never, not in this life or the next, would he
take my side. Even in heaven, the Traynors and their kind

would be seated in a more exclusive part of the establishment. Even in heaven, I'd be fitted with the wrong kind of wings. Theirs would be snowy-white, of moderate size and impeccable grooming. Mine would draggle and moult.

Then I thought of Cynthia, who would stroll into this little gathering and blow it to bits with her beauty. Cynthia would have beautiful wings, iridescent, flaunting wings. Wings like an angel's in an Abbott Thayer painting, wings that filled a sky. As for Harry, Harry's wings would be the brightest blue, edged in gold. He'd use them to do all sorts of zippy aerial tricks, cartwheels and somersaults, while these well-bred seraphim looked on in disapproval.

I looked at Philip. He'd have tidy grey wings, like a pigeon's.

'I'm going,' I said to Philip. He didn't turn. I nudged his elbow.

'I'm *going*.'

'*What*?'

'I can't take any more of this.'

He gave an irritated sigh.

'Another half-hour,' he muttered, and turned back around without waiting for my answer. Now the room wavered in a mist of rage: the nuns in their prissy sportswear, the circle of insurance lobbyists, the trays upon trays of pear-topped vanilla ice cream the waiters were bringing from dim warm parts behind the wall.

I grabbed my evening purse (in which I always carried cab fare, for my mother had taught me well) and left them all there, as it turned out I'd always wanted to do.

Chapter XIV

In soap operas, women never have to tell men they love them. In soap operas, the way is made clear. The couple is thrown dramatically together by a tornado, an arsonist's torch, a storm that isolates them in a mountain cabin. On *Covington Heights*, the chief of police, Holden Reilly, had told April Dunning he loved her when they had been trapped by a mud slide in an underground chamber. He had said, 'Even if these are our last hours, I wouldn't be anywhere else than here with you.' All April had to do was let him pull her to him, sink with him to the ground, and fade to black.

Telling Harry I'd left Philip would be easy. Telling him I loved him and wanted to bring our connection out into the daylight would be full of pitfalls.

For Harry hadn't said he loved me. Men always liked some assurance before using that word, I told myself. Harry had been hurt before. I could be the first to say it for once. Would it kill me? I would go to him and declare myself. I had never declared myself before. I had always been the declaree.

So I let it go for a few weeks, for nearly a month. October ended, November began, and still I was seeing Harry as if I were meeting him on the sly. I began to worry that part of me loved the sneaking around, loved feeling like the focal point for *two* men, feeling like the heart of the plot. Old movies are like that. There are always at least two guys who want the

beautiful heroine – like *The Philadelphia Story*, where Cary
Grant and Jimmy Stewart (*and* the boring fiancé!) all want
Katherine Hepburn while she floats around wearing great
clothes and worrying whether she's so rich and gorgeous people always think of her as an ice princess? Do too many men
adore her without really *knowing* her? We should all have
such problems.

I knew I had to chance it with Harry sooner or later. And
when week followed week and Philip and I didn't patch it up,
our split began to seem like fact to me, a true break rather than
another lovers' quarrel. Harry had to know if only because
someone (like Cynthia) might tell him before I did. So one
night when we were lying in bed and he had asked with
attempted casualness where Philip was, I said, equally
offhanded, 'I've left Philip.'

'Left him?' He didn't look at me. He was reading the sports
section. It is hard to deliver momentous news to a man who's
absorbed in an account of the Celtics' lousy season.

'You two had a fight?' he said finally, turning a page but
not putting the paper down.

'Sort of.'

'Does he know about you and me?'

'Not yet. I told him my marrying him would be a mistake.'

Philip had shown up at my door an hour after I left the
Hibernian dinner.

'You don't really like me,' I'd said. 'You never really liked
me, Philip. You only wanted me against your better judg-
ment. You think loving me is some sort of weakness.'

'What are you talking about?' Philip said.

'You're always correcting me. Like the other day when
you told me I was too effusive with your mother. *Anyone*
would look effusive next to your mother. She never unbends.
But all you could do was criticize me.'

'All I said was …'

'All you can ever say is what I'm doing wrong, you know that.'

'We'll talk about this later, when you've calmed down,' he said.

'I am calm!' I had screamed. Shortly after, he'd left. He'd be back, I'd thought. He didn't even take me seriously enough to believe he was being dumped. And sure enough, there had been flowers (orchids, which always smelled like funerals to me) and heated phone calls, and an exhausting scene in my living room in which I recounted the slights and grudges of the last year and Philip told me I was crazy. This is the problem with bottling things up, of course. By the time you get the courage to mention what's bothering you, most people don't remember the incident that upset you in the first place. Philip had finally walked out, shaking his head, and I'd felt balked of a final, cleansing fight.

'So what do you think?' I said to Harry.

'About what?'

'About Marty Conlon's jump shot. About us, for God's sake.'

'Well, why not see how it goes?'

'How do you think it's going?'

'Very well.'

I rose and went into the other room, where I walked around straightening pillows and shelving books and fuming. It seemed to me I deserved credit for breaking it off with Philip, and here was Harry acting as if I'd simply cleaned out the bedroom closet instead of saying goodbye to the man I'd promised to marry.

After ten minutes I heard the paper rustle and Harry walked out.

'I hate announcements,' he said. 'I'm sorry. I'm really glad we won't have to sneak around anymore.'

We kissed, we made love, and the moment with its dangers

and unrealized decisions passed. Two weeks later we were at
the zoo, where Harry liked to go walking. It was four-thirty on
a November afternoon. Harry was playing hooky from the
office and Cynthia had offered to close the shop. She'd been
delighted I had broken it off with Philip.

Before I met Harry I hated the zoo. I hated the smell, the
animals cooped up in cages, the hordes of tourists who sometimes seemed to deserve being caged more than the creatures
they viewed. But Harry made it new, as he made so many
other places new. He liked to watch the monkeys flirt and
chatter and swing high above the crowd. He liked to saunter
down the birdwalk. He liked to see the ducks dive for food
and the panther pacing dangerously. He pointed out the
golden lion tamarinds, who were living in outside cages in
preparation for a return to freedom in the jungles of Brazil.

We were watching the elephants when he delivered the
news.

The elephant house stinks of hay and elephant manure, a
cabbagy-sulfur smell. Harry was leaning over the railing,
absorbed in some maneuvering of the female elephant's trunk
and an inner tube.

'Evolution is amazing,' he said to me. 'Imagine the first
ape with an opposable thumb. Imagine how incredible that
must have seemed. To be able to grab things all of a sudden.'

'Harry, you've been quiet all day.'

'This is difficult to say,' he said.

My stomach began a long elevator ride, plunging from
floor to floor, plunging so slowly and sickeningly that it
seemed it would never hit ground. Your stomach always
knows before the rest of you does.

'I meant to tell you this before. I should have told you,' he
said. 'Nancy's been calling me.'

'And?'

'She's been wondering if we did the right thing.'

'A little late, isn't it.'

'Well, that's just the ... just the issue. She doesn't want to call it quits.'

'And what did you tell her?'

But I knew what he'd told her.

'I told her I had to think about it. We've been writing each other. She calls me once a week.'

That horrible matrimonial 'we'. The air in here was so stale and muggy. A child brushed his cotton candy against my bare arm. The stickiness of it felt like running into a spiderweb.

'Try to understand,' said Harry. 'She feels that you don't just walk out on a marriage because of some bad times. You don't just throw away five years together.'

'The other guy left her, didn't he.'

'He walked out. The asshole.'

'That doesn't mean you have to go back to her.'

'She's a mess,' he said. 'How could I tell her I wouldn't even think about it?'

'You say, I'm sorry Nancy. I'm here if you need a shoulder to cry on. But I'm seeing someone else now.'

But he wouldn't say that, couldn't say that. His face told me, his face that had the 'wish I could be anywhere but here look' men's faces have when they're telling you some awful truth.

'You can't go back to her,' I said. 'It'll kill you. She'll have you beaten down before you know it.'

'I'm transferring back to the New York office,' he said, as if I hadn't spoken. 'Her idea is that we'd give it a trial run.'

'I can't believe this,' I said.

'I'm sorry,' said Harry. 'I'm supposed to be in New York on Tuesday.'

He looked miserable, but I was too stunned, hurt and angry to find an ounce of pity for him.

'Nancy was always the one who counted,' I said.

'I can't leave her in the lurch. I can't do it. Don't ask me to.'

'No, God forbid you behave like your father; leave a cold woman. Heavens no! God forbid you have a little happiness of your own.'

'I'm so sorry,' said Harry. 'You saved my life this summer.'

'You *lied* to me,' I said. 'You made me think you loved me. You acted like a man in love.'

'*I* lied? Maybe I'm letting you down – I know I'm letting you down – but I am not the liar in this situation. All these weeks you never said the first word to end it with your precious upper-class boyfriend with the corner office and the snooty expectations and the impressive family history.'

'I might have if you'd given me one encouraging sign, one sign that I was more than just a rebound fling.'

'You know you were more than that.'

'Were? You're already talking about me in the past tense?'

He gave me a look of helpless apology. The more helpless and apologetic he looked the angrier I got, especially since I knew I had no technical right to be angry. Harry had made me no promises and had asked me for none. Remembering this made me angrier than ever.

'You should have trusted what we had together,' I said. 'You should have pushed me a little. I'd have been braver if you'd have pushed me.'

'I'm sorry,' he said again, then he said, 'I do love you. Sometimes you just have to try to do the right thing. You know I'd rather stay here with you.'

'Then why don't you? You think it makes me feel any better knowing that you want to be here with me and you're leaving anyway? You think that's a consolation?'

'I have to be able to tell myself I tried with Nancy.'

'Fuck Nancy,' I said.

A family of six was pressing in the back of us, jostling for a space by the railing. I hung on to the railing. The cold iron felt good against my hot wrists. My whole life men had been saying they loved me and then getting on a plane.

'Get out of here, Harry. I'm going to stand right here and you're going to walk away so I don't have to look at your fucking face anymore. You damn coward.'

He touched my shoulder. I just stood there, trying not to blink so I wouldn't cry.

Then he left. I told him to leave and like a patsy he walked away. No fight at all. Going back to the cactus, the turtles, the bottled water. Going back to the Unitarians and rice cakes. Nothing made sense at all.

That night I bought a bottle of white wine and drank the whole thing like medicine. I was truly my mother's daughter.

When I was good and drunk, I played the Tom Waits tape again. I played 'Downtown Train' over and over until my neighbor banged on the wall.

> If I was the one
> [*sang Tom Waits in the gravelly voice of exhausted love*]
> You chose to be your only one
> Can't you hear me now, can't you hear me now
> Will I see you tonight
> On a downtown train
> All my tears, all my tears, fall like rain
> On a downtown train

'To hell with you,' I shouted at my neighbor and banged right back, knocking down several pieces of plaster that had been impending from the dining room ceiling for weeks.

'I hate men,' I said aloud, staggering around my apartment because I was too mad at Harry to sit down. 'Men are such fuckers.'

The photos in their pewter frames regarded me. My mother leaning against a lamppost on her one and only trip to New Orleans. Cynthia languishing in a Rita Hayworth mermaid dress and Veronica Lake hair. Philip in front of the family sailboat, windblown and boyish. My father and mother dancing at Annette's wedding, looking for once like a couple in love. I had kept that picture because sometimes, if I looked at them out of the corner of my eye, I could pretend they'd been happy.

I tried calling my father's house to talk to Cynthia, but all I got was a busy signal. So I just kept drinking and reflecting on the betrayals of men, a subject on which I was a minor expert. Men were a trap door at your feet, a falling safe, arsenic in your tea. You could never count on them, not the best of them. Beyond irony or impartiality, I gathered the evidence in my head: the faithless Simon Moore, and all of Cynthia's beautiful heartless scoundrels. The insubstantial ghost-men of my twenties, the ones who were always producing a ticket to somewhere else just as you began to get used to them. The ones who *didn't* do you the favor of leaving, like Philip with his critical eye, his unsparing judgments. My father, with his harsh voice, his loud overbearing ways, his complete belief in his own rightness. Harry, who had seemed to be the one good apple in this wormy bunch, Harry who turned out to be the squirreliest of them all.

Nothing was enough for men, I decided. Not love, not devotion, not tenderness, not riotous passion. They'd rather be hurting themselves with some cruel woman than loving and being loved by women who didn't measure out their affection with a teaspoon. No wonder all the fairy tales were full of unattainable princesses – men didn't like any other kind. Once you were attained, you were chicken feed. I remembered, with that clear flash of memory that comes to you when you're tipsy, a tale by the Brothers Grimm my mother had read me once, about a princess on a glass hill whose suitors had to climb the hill to win her. That was men all over, I thought. Flocking to that hill, hurling themselves against that slippery glass.

I got out *Little Women* and read the chapter where Beth announces she's dying, then the chapter where she dies. I always did that on overwrought occasions.

'Sometimes I think I'll be homesick for you even in heaven,' Beth told Jo. That was how I felt for Harry: homesick. I sobbed all over the page, but that didn't matter because it was already blistered with the tears of earlier break-ups.

The next morning my temples felt as if someone were tying my capillaries into slip knots. My mouth was parched and musty, the skin under my eyes yellowish and puffy.

In the old days I could have called in sick to the Agency, but there was a shop now, with our name freshly stenciled on the door. I took four aspirins and put some cucumber slices on my eyes to soothe the puffiness. Cynthia was coming in that morning. She would be on my side. Her comments would cut Harry down to his proper size, the size of a selfish little troll.

But when I got to the shop it wasn't sisterly balm that was waiting for me. I heard voices, one of them Cynthia's, as I trudged up the stairs, which had never seemed more unreasonably steep. There, sitting on the big old sofa with Cynthia, was Simon Moore in person, and he was holding my sister's hand and feeding her bits of croissant and sips of cafe latte as if she were a baby bird.

His face had the strange unreality of a face you've seen often on television, as if his television self were the real Simon and this self in the flesh were just a pale imitation. And he was pale indeed, with dark circles under his eyes. He was

wearing a leather jacket and suede half-boots which would
have looked foppish on anyone else, a black sweater and
black jeans. In the winter sunshine, he seemed an apparition
of the night.

'Finally you're here,' said Cynthia.

Simon rose and shook my hand. I tried to remember he was
from Toledo, because the impression he instantly gave was of
an English public school education.

'Nice to see you again,' said Simon. It was like hearing
Heathcliff make pleasantries.

'Simon and Delia are getting divorced,' Cynthia
announced. 'For real. He caught the train last night and surprised me.'

She held out her left hand, where I saw a tasteful square-cut
diamond framed by aquamarines. There was an expression of
humble rapture on the guy's face, a real Garden of Eden look.

'We're getting married,' said Simon. 'At last.'

'I'm glad for you,' I said, eying him suspiciously, this matinee idol who had kept my sister waiting for two whole years.
Then I sat down in our only armchair.

'I thought I would show Simon what we've done,' said
Cynthia.

They billed and cooed their way through the shop. Simon
kept saying, 'But this is great, Cynthia, really great. God,
you're talented.' Once Cynthia turned to me and said, 'You're
getting a cold, aren't you,' but that was all she noticed of my
mood. When you are down and out of love, Fate is sure to
flaunt the happiest pair She can find in front of you. It didn't
help that my sister and Simon looked like the glamorous couples in automobile ads, the ones who stand in front of their
Mercedes at the edge of the Big Sur or in the driveway of an
immaculate mansion. They radiated health and happiness. I
hated them.

'This place has an air all its own,' said Simon.

'You should have seen it when I got here,' said Cynthia.

Through it all I kept expecting someone from Simon's show to stroll in, Edwin or Charmaine or the new character, a vixen named Flame Saddler. Flame Saddler had red hair and a slutty wardrobe. She was the long-lost daughter of Dr. Moira Bowden, and she'd already seduced two male characters: bad boy Roger Campion and minister Alden Holmes. They were simply appetizers, however. Her real target would eventually be Brice Covington, the man sitting here in our shop drinking coffee and holding my sister's hand. Couples in love did that. They touched. Right in front of you, on purpose, to tell you what a solitary unlovable person you were. I drank my coffee and downed an antihistamine. Soon I'd have a lovely buzz that would see me through the day.

'So Simon insisted on meeting Daddy last night,' said Cynthia.

'Daddy who?'

'He woke him up at three a.m. to ask for his blessing.'

'I'm kind of old-fashioned,' said Simon in that classy, resonant voice.

'Dad was eating right out of his hand,' Cynthia said.

It enraged me, the thought of my father and Simon sitting around the kitchen table, my dad drinking whatever beer had been on sale that week, Simon drinking whatever Byronic heros drank these days, chumming around as if the guy were the picture of manly virtue. Cynthia got engaged and the red carpet was rolled out. I got engaged and received warnings of eternal damnation.

'He took Simon to see his workshop,' said Cynthia.

My father had never taken Philip to see his workshop, a musty cavern in what was once our garage, where my father tinkered with discarded auto engines and broken radios, cut the stakes for his vegetable garden and in spring grew tomato seedlings in tiny paper pots. This workshop was the only

place my father had ever been in a good mood for any length
of time. You could sometimes hear his voice floating up the
basement stairs, singing 'Those Wedding Bells are Breaking
Up That Old Gang of Mine' or 'The Big Rock Candy
Mountain'. When we were children, we were allowed to stand
quietly, passing him a hammer or cranking the vise. He never
took strangers into his workshop. But Simon he took.

'So you're getting married? That's great. That's wonderful.'

'In April,' said Cynthia, as if it had never been in doubt. 'I
want you to be my maid of honor. We're going to have a big
wedding. A great big wedding.'

'All our friends,' said Simon.

'Hundreds,' said my sister. 'And I'm going to wear that old
thirties wedding gown I bought for twenty bucks at the Value
Thrift. And you're going to wear ...'

She fell silent, contemplating what I would wear.

'We told you first after your father,' said Simon, beaming
on me.

'That's great. Thank you.'

'What we thought was we'd all go out to dinner tonight.
Me and Simon and you and Harry. Because,' my sister
paused, 'we're going back to New York tomorrow. Simon's
got to get back and he won't go without me.'

Lovers said those sorts of things. 'He won't go without
me.' Men had always been perfectly able to go without *me*. If
you were beautiful and heedless and knew there would
always be men to love you, men would stay and stay, howling
under your window like stray dogs. Like that line from the
Gospel about more being given to those who already had. I
knew these thoughts were unkind and uncharitable, but there
they were. I hated this dog-in-the-manger side of myself.

I said, 'Harry's not here. He's going back to New York
too.'

'Back to New York?'

Now Cynthia focused on me, her lovely blue eyes narrowing.

I began folding a pile of cashmere sweaters. 'He's going back with Nancy. A trial reunion, isn't that funny? Most couples have a trial separation.'

Simon tactfully wandered away to a display of strapless tulle evening gowns hung in bunches, like bouquets of carnations, against the big bay window. Cynthia had arranged them there. Cynthia had arranged everything. Now she was going, part of the mass exodus on the Yankee Clipper for cooler Northern climes. If I had been cool like Nancy, I thought now, Harry would still be here.

'That asshole,' said Cynthia. 'That pure complete Grade A asshole.'

'You win some, you lose some.'

She put her arm around me and said, 'Are you all right?'

'I'm more worried about the store than stupid Harry,' I said, but I didn't fool Cynthia.

'You'll do fine with the store.'

'I'm glad one of us got what she wants,' I said. 'You need help with the wedding, you call me.'

'You'd hate that,' said Cynthia. 'Francesca is already making plans. But I'll call you anyway.'

Before she left, she gave me a new lipstick in a shade called Raisin Spice that she'd bought the day before. 'You could go with more brown in your lipstick,' she said. Then she followed Simon down the stairs. I watched them go, and said a Hail Mary for my sister's happiness because habit is hard to break, and then I turned back into my store and began adding up that week's receipts. The numbers said what they'd been saying for weeks now – Cynthia's had a better-than-fighting chance.

Chapter XV

That winter the weather was so bad it became a topic sufficient unto itself. People compared notes about car accidents and broken ankles, tree branches falling and boiler pipes freezing. Snow came early in November, followed by two freak storms that left the streets treacherous with invisible black ice. I trudged from day to day.

There's something you learn once you're over thirty. You learn that surviving is a matter of putting time between you and what hurt you, that time makes you stronger and tougher in spite of yourself. When you're younger people tell you this but you don't want to believe them. When you're older you take consolation in the fact. I had always wondered if the people who gave up, the ones who turned to razor blades and pill bottles, were the ones who couldn't hang on another day or week. They were the people who slipped out of the gracious hold of Time.

Over the next weeks I did all the things Cynthia and I had planned to do, although I felt as shaky as if I were recovering from typhoid. Cynthia had bought a box of white plaster cherubs from a cut-rate home decorating store before she left. Her idea had been to hang them at the top of the four exposed water pipes in the corners of the front room. I painted the pipes white and then went to a specialty fabric store and discovered wired, gold-mesh ribbon, which I wound around the pipes like Maypole ribbon. Then I sewed the angel's hanging loops right to the wire and concealed the sewn spot with clusters of ribbon rosettes. The effect, as Rafaella commented, was 'very rococco'. At some point, I thought, I would paint the ceilings the palest cerulean blue with floating white clouds, and make the peach on our walls a little paler, with a scrubbed, washed look I had admired in some Venetian palazzo I'd seen in *Architectural Digest*.

Some wonderful clothes came in that fall, partly from word of mouth and partly because I was willing to go further for consignments if a phone call or tip promised a good haul. I would pay Rafaella to watch the shop every Wednesday and set out in my '64 Dodge Dart, trundling all over the countryside.

A retired librarian in Hagerstown entrusted me with boxes of things she hadn't worn since the fifties, including eight cashmere twinsets in mint condition. Often the moths beat you to cashmere, and there would be heartbreaking tiny holes. In Middleburg, a too-young widower stood with a look of profound relief as I loaded suitcases of his wife's wardrobe, which included everything from Eileen Fisher to Albert Nipon, into my trunk and back seat. He just handed the suitcases to me. He had not looked inside them since he packed them up the week after she died. She had been dead of breast cancer for two years, but he couldn't bring himself to throw out her clothes and they had no daughters.

He said he was going to give his consignment money to a cancer foundation. I told him that I thought practical action was a real cure for grief and that I'd do the same with my cut.

In Wilmington a woman who had lost fifty pounds at Weight Watchers joyfully handed over her size fourteen cocktail dresses, business suits and tailored slacks – and I knew just the customer for them, a restaurateur who didn't

care that she was a size 14 and looked wonderful in everything she wore.

These pilgrimages cheered me up. But at night, when I got
home, after frantic cleaning or vacuuming or book straightening, after all the physical activities that distracted me, there was
always the half-hour after I'd brushed my teeth and washed my
face and put down my book and turned out the light. In that half
hour it seemed Harry walked away from me again and again.

You can't choose where you belong any more than you can
choose your talents or the color of your eyes. I loved Harry in
the same way that I was flat-chested, the same way I hated
nutmeg, the same way I'd inherited my mother's downslop-
ing eyelids. My lucid, consoling brain knew that I would
someday find another man I would love very much, maybe
more than I'd loved Harry. But the thought of that man made
me feel desperately lonely for Harry. I wanted him, not some
new love, not even a better love.

At the Church of the Infant Martyrs when I was a girl, that
fierce old priest Father Flynn used to quote St. Paul's famous
passage: 'Now we see as through a glass darkly, then we shall
see clear.' A believer whose heart was already in the afterlife,
he had urged his parishioners to look forward to death. With a
child's knowledge of what is worth wanting and what we're
told we should, I knew that even if a dazzling clear-edged
heaven were guaranteed, I would rather stay here, among my
familiar earthly things.

What is real? Is it the real you in the bathtub sobbing after
the breakup, or is it the real you a year later – so tough, so
strong, with a new piece of scar tissue you might even show
off. I didn't want to remember Harry as someone I'd gotten
over, or joke about him five years from now as some loser I
was lucky to escape from. I didn't want to look forward to a
time when I would ache over him only on rainy days, as if old
love were a nagging rheumatism.

When I was ninety-five I'd think sometimes of Harry and miss him as keenly as I did right that minute. I knew about grief. I could go for months without thinking of my grandfather, and then at the Italian market when I saw an old paisan with tough weatherbeaten skin like his I would miss him as if he'd just left me. Or when I saw some classic real gold earrings at a department store, my hand would go to my wallet to buy them for my finicky mother.

How awful to consign people to memory. My mother, who had disappeared before my eyes. My grandfather, who had forgotten me years before he died, who had forgotten everything and trembled like a little child. Philip, who had a cool elastic heart and could love one woman as easily as another, who probably suffered little over our parting.

To avoid these sorrowful nights I wore myself out with sheer activity. As the weeks went by and Christmas approached, life became almost bearable again.

Chapter XVI

Over the holidays, Cynthia's did a brisk business in formal-wear. Sometimes women were a little embarrassed to be buying their party dresses secondhand, but most of my customers were thrilled to get a bargain. After all, you paid through the nose for formals and then wore them twice a year. Cynthia's had it any way a customer's unfulfilled prom night dreams led her – sequinned tunic tops over widelegged chiffon pants, true ball gowns with crinolines and miles of taffeta skirt, strapless velvets or metallic halter necks. Whether you wanted to wrap yourself up delectably in bright red satin or make a dangerous entrance in a white silk tux cut down to there, Cynthia's could oblige.

Cynthia herself came down without Simon for three days in early December, to work out wedding plans. But Francesca saw more of her than I did. For the first time in their lives, they were getting along. Cynthia was organizing her wedding with a military efficiency, and Francesca was a master sergeant of details. Into Cynthia's wedding Francesca poured all the logistical ability she hadn't been able to exercise in her own shoestring teenage marriage.

Annette and Francesca were going to be bridesmaids and I was maid of honor – like all of us, Cynthia didn't have many women friends. Actor buddies of Simon's were going to be the ushers, and his brother would be best man. Only a few

other people from the show were asked, since Cynthia said
she didn't want her wedding to look like one of Brice
Covington's.

'You're right,' I said. 'You want him to know it's for real
this time.'

'Oh, he'll know all right.'

The wedding was planned to coincide with a brief disappearance by Brice, with plot details yet to be worked out.
Somehow, the writers would engineer a diasaster so that
Simon could marry my sister and take a four-day honeymoon
in Nova Scotia.

'What happened to him when he married Delia?'

'That was when he was being held hostage by that Belgian
drug-manufacturing family so that he wouldn't reveal what
they were doing to the town's water supply.'

'Oh right. In the secret vault under Covington Bank and
Trust.'

The wedding would be held in New York. Cynthia had
lived there for years, and it had always been her spiritual
home. Besides, no one wanted to contemplate the spectacle of
Cynthia's actor friends and theater connections blinking
under the open sky of her birth city, or having allergic attacks
in reaction to its excessive vegetation. They would suffer
deeply, whereas our family would find New York an adven-
ture. And there were ample connections on my father's
mother's side in Brooklyn and New Jersey to provide rooms
for every last third cousin.

The nuptial mass was going to be performed in the small
church of St. Rita on Amsterdam Avenue, with a reception
afterwards at the Graham, a Gilded Age hotel Cynthia had
picked for its faded splendor and in-house catering (the guests
would be choosing between salmon croquettes and stuffed
capon). As she'd told me, Cynthia was going to wear the wedding dress from the 1930s that she'd found on one of our thrift

store runs. It was a slinky, heavy ivory satin, with a wide boat neck, fitted bodice and cap sleeves. The skirt was sown in eight separate panels that fit close to the body to the knees, then swirled and pooled around Cynthia's ankles. It was in the process of being cleaned and lovingly mended by a firm that specialized in restoring bridal gowns. Cynthia's headdress would be a white satin Juliet cap with a veil attached to the back. She wanted to make sure people could see her face the entire time. Being swathed in tulle and unrecogniz-able was not her idea of a dream entrance.

There was no veil for Cynthia to inherit from my mother, and no dress either. My mother had given them to an order of nuns. Back in those days, postulants making their final vows wore wedding dresses to show they were brides of Christ, and charitably minded young Catholic women donated their wed-ding dresses for the purpose.

'What does it say that she was willing to give her wedding dress to a convent only six months after she got married?' I asked Cynthia while we ate beef stew and crusty Italian rolls in the back room of the shop.

'It says she was a good Catholic,' said Francesca, who never seemed to leave Cynthia's side and had bought a bulging vinyl folder in which she kept hard copies of all the wedding data, which was also stored on her home computer. Today she was poring over a list of prices for flowers. Flowers cost more than I'd ever dreamed of, and all the wed-ding expenses would come out of Cynthia's pocket, out of years of modeling fees, including the ten thousand she'd made dancing as a showgirl in Tokyo. She had been deter-mined not to take a penny from Simon, nor from my father, although he'd have mortgaged the house to pull it off. Luckily, *RosePetal*'s was shooting another catalogue, and a calendar too. In this calendar Cynthia was also a bride, appearing for the month of June in a pillbox hat with a netting veil, white corset, white silk tap pants, and a pair of ivory go-go boots.

'But Mom wasn't a good Catholic,' I said. 'She never really caught on. I mean, she thought you could skip Mass and go to the coffee shop instead and God would understand. She only went to Confession during Lent. And she taught us all those hymns from the Baptist hymnal.'

'"I Come to the Garden Alone",' put in Cynthia.

'I Come to the Garden Alone' was one of my mother's favorite hymns. The words went:

> I come to the garden alone
> While the dew is still on the roses
> And the voice I hear
> Whispering in my ear
> The sweetest tale discloses
>
> And He walks with me
> And He talks with me
> And He tells me I am His own
> And the joy we share as we tarry there
> No other has ever known.

Now, only a Protestant would imagine that Jesus would stroll around a garden with you like a lover. Any Catholic girl knows better. Catholic girls were told of Fatima and Lourdes, of Joan of Arc, who heard voices and was burned at the stake. Tormented hermits. Virgin martyrs like Sts. Cecelia and Agatha and Agnes and Catherine, who got their heads chopped off or their eyes gouged out or were scalded to death or had their limbs pulled apart by horses. Consider St. Maria Goretti, the big cheese of girl saints when I was growing up, who had preferred multiple stab wounds to carnal knowledge of a man. That was the kind of personal contact Catholics had with the divine. My mother, like other Protestants, imagined God took a benign interest in her life. Catholics knew that if God started noticing your existence, you could expect to suffer big time.

'She had the priest in every day when she was at Georgetown,' said Francesca.

'She liked the attention,' I said.

'Who are you to say? How do you know what was going through her mind then? When was the last time *you* went to church?'

'None of your business,' I said. Actually, I went once a month to light candles in the St. Francis chapel at St. Matthew's cathedral. The chapel was always empty. I would put five dollars in the offering box and light ten candles. On the walls of the chapel are the praises to God's creations that St. Francis wrote when he was ill at San Damiano. He praised the moon, the sun, and the stars, the plants and trees. St. Francis had loved God's world. My favorite praise read, 'Praise to thee, Brother Fire, who gives us warmth and maketh light the night/Thou art lovely and pleasant, mighty and strong.' This praise always made me think of Harry.

Paul was doing the wedding photos. There would also be a photographer from Soap Stories Weekly. A swing band would play at the reception, with their own little tiered bandstand.

'Just like Ricky Ricardo's band on *I Love Lucy*', I said.

'It's not a bit like Ricky Ricardo's band,' said Francesca.

Cynthia had decided that after the wedding she was going to go into business – she didn't know where and she didn't know what.

'You're giving up acting?' I said. Francesca beamed approval.

'Face it, I gave up acting a long time ago. I can still do

community stuff and off-off Broadway. But I'm tired. It's time to try something else.'

'You were great in *Lend Me A Tenor*.'

'But I didn't get Maggie, I got the vamp part. And the theater was in Brooklyn Heights.'

'What sort of business?' asked Francesca, who was now flipping through a book of place settings.

'I'm thinking about a lot of things – maybe secondhand furniture. Maybe real estate. I have no idea. I just know I like making money.'

I said, 'You can open up a Cynthia's in New York.'

'Maybe I should open a Diana's.'

The bridesmaid's dresses were surprisingly beautiful, the kindest bridesmaids' dresses I'd ever seen. They were made of chiffon all in misty colors. There was a mauvy fog-gray for Annette that set off her big blue eyes and glinty-blonde hair, a misty pale gold for Francesca, and for me a cream-colored one just one shade less white than Cynthia's dress. The style was blissfully simple, just an ankle-length silk slip with a sleeveless chiffon dress over it. The dresses fell straight from a scoop neck and were bias cut, to cling enough to look sinuous without looking trashy. With them we'd wear long ropes of costume pearls.

The whole effect was 'very Great Gatsby', as Francesca said, although she also insisted that we would all be cold wearing sleeveless dresses in late April. Our hats were cream straw, from Rafaella. Annette's was trimmed with just one spray of palest silver roses, Francesca's was loaded with golden roses, and mine had one red rose pinning back the wide brim, over my left eye. Annette and I would have flat, cream ivory satin slippers, Annette's with an ankle strap, mine with a crisscross. Francesca would wear cream satin pumps, to even out our heights. I had cut my hair when Harry disappeared. It was now in a twenties bob that I had to admit was very flattering under the wide picture hat.

Cynthia and Simon were bluffing their way through Pre-Cana. Luckily, the Brooklyn couple supposed to be their mentors was more interested in upcoming events on Covington Heights than in outlining the pitfalls of the married state. Bridget confided to Cynthia that she had been on the Pill for years, and Danny asked Simon what it was like working with dozens of beautiful girls every day. They even allowed Simon and my sister to take the Pre-Cana questionnaire (supposed to predict stress points in your marriage) in the same room. Brice Covington, of course, would never take a premarital questionnaire. Maybe he would have gone through fewer wives if he had. Then again, maybe not.

My father, of course, was incredibly thrilled about Cynthia's marriage to a television star. He had even begun watching Covington Heights, and when he missed a day he would call me for an update. Until he was seven he had lived in a tiny village sixty miles from Naples where no one had electricity or running water. Television was still a miracle to him. Along the mantle now were a new row of photographs: Cynthia and Simon on the porch swing, Cynthia and Simon admiring my father's tomato garden, Cynthia and Simon holding hands in front of the painting of my mother, which hung in the dining room.

'You ever hear from that Philip?' my father asked when he called to see if April and the police commissioner had found the secret drawer in his desk yet, the one that revealed who was leaking information to the press in the Moresby case.

'No, Dad. I dumped him, remember? He's a little mad at me.'

'Well, maybe you should think about giving him a call. You're not getting any younger.'

I knew what had prompted this. Desiree on *Covington*

Heights was getting a face lift. The actress who played her was all of twenty-two. The doctor who was giving her the face lift was a charlatan named Cleve Saunders. He was going to scar her so badly that her whole appearance would have to be altered at a Swiss clinic, thus freeing the actress to take a role in an upcoming disaster film called *Cyclone III: The Climax*. It also would explain why the new Desiree would look completely different.

'I don't see you asking Mrs. Petrocelli out to dinner.'

'That's a different story,' said my father. Mrs. Petrocelli was the widow of his best friend. She could play a mean game of poker and her linguini with sausage made grown men cry with joy.

'I tell you what, Dad, I'll think about getting married the day you think about dating again.'

'I had a long happy marriage.'

Well, a long one at least.

'Dad, at your age the ratio is entirely with you, you know that? You could be swimming in women.'

'I have some chicken soup on the stove,' said my father, and rang off.

During her visit Cynthia also gave me intelligence on Harry. She said, 'I saw him the other night. At a cocktail party. He looked miserable.'

'Was his wife there?'

'Yeah. She was standing next to him practically the whole time. For your information, she has very thick ankles.'

'What was she wearing?'

'She was wearing this black matronly thing you could tell she paid a million bucks for at Neiman Marcus. Just a plain black A-line you could pick up for eighty dollars at Filene's. And these big wooden beads shaped like animals. From Kenya or God knows where. She wore her hair up in a chignon.'

'Is she prettier than me?'

'Oh my God no. Not half as pretty as you.'

'She's not prettier than me and she's mean to him. Would someone please explain this to me?'

'Men are idiots.'

'That's it? That's the explanation?'

'I'm sorry, babe.'

Cynthia had apologized a million times for introducing me to Harry.

'You didn't force me to sleep with him, Cynthia.' That was how I was referring to it now. Harry was just some guy I'd slept with. But Cynthia knew better.

'At least he helped you get rid of Philip.'

Harry had asked about the wedding, Cynthia said, when she had maneuvered him away to the bar. He had asked if I'd be in it. She had not invited him, of course. Harry may have once pried her residuals out of the hands of the Taco Town people, but her sister came first, she had informed me the week the invitations went out. Unless I *wanted* him to be invited. Which, I assured her, I didn't. And immediately wondered if all it would take was for Harry to see me again. If our eyes met across a crowded church, me in that great dress and Harry in his rumpled blue suit, would that pull as real as gravity start working again? Then I envisioned Harry walking into St. Rita's with Nancy on his arm, looking contented and a little patronizing, as married couples did at weddings. No, I told Cynthia, no Harry at the wedding.

'I said, of course you'd be in it, you were maid of honor. I told him about your dress, and then I told him about my dress.'

Harry probably hadn't been able to get a word in edgewise. Why should he care what I was doing with myself anymore? He'd chosen Nancy. I had learned this much in my screwed-up love life: the women men chose weren't accidents. A man, in the end, wound up with the woman he deep down wanted to be with. And if Harry was tied to Nancy by duty and family guilt, something in him embraced that duty and that family guilt. Maybe Nancy was his ticket to virtue. Or maybe deep at heart he was comfortable only with mean cold women like his mother. Served him right, then.

But I was really looking for signs that he'd loved me at all, at any time, if the person I'd been with was really Harry or an impersonation. After someone was gone you could never know if he'd loved you. You went over and over what he had said, how he had looked, searching for clues. But that bright sureness of love slipped away forever.

'I told him your shop was going great. He said, I always knew she'd make the shop a success. Tell her I'm glad for her. But he didn't look glad. He looked miserable, absolutely haggard, and then five minutes later Miss Ice-Pussy comes up to us and takes him away. She didn't leave his side the rest of the night.' This happened a lot to Cynthia, of course. Wives who saw her in a corner with their husbands were prone to swoop down and drag their spouses off.

'I hope he is miserable. I hope he's walking down the street and a crane drops a big steel beam on his head. I hope he falls down an elevator shaft. I hope Nancy never has sex with him again.'

'Not having sex with her would be no punishment,' said Cynthia.

There was a huge family Christmas, which Cynthia missed because she was back in New York with Simon. I gave my brothers gift certificates to a record store, Annette and Paul a new comforter, my father more picture frames, and Francesca perfume. She gave me three pairs of thermal socks. During dessert, Annette's husband Paul and Francesca's husband

Jerry and my father argued about the Balkans, shouting at each other and banging the table. This was routine. The kids played with my father's Lionel train set in the basement. I left early, not helping Francesca with the dishes, which she mentioned first thing the next time I saw her.

Chapter XVII

In January I began to date again. I went to dinner with an ex-Peace Corps volunteer who talked the whole evening about his two years in Botswana. He even brought pictures of the cement hut he lived in and himself teaching English to native children. I went to the movies with a C.P.A., one of Jerry's friends. I visited the National Gallery with an art historian who took me from painting to painting, lecturing on the Cinquecento. Every man who asked me out I gave three dates, just to give myself a chance to fall for their good points and stop comparing them to Harry. Each time I would tell them the chemistry wasn't right, and sigh with huge relief when I regained my cozy apartment, where no one wanted to tell me about Third World agriculture or the joys of the Internet. For while it can be adorable to hear the man you love going on about batting averages or quantum physics, a charmless man who is bent on playing teacher is as annoying as the voice of a bus station announcer.

The ice storms kept coming one after another, so that we all had to walk as gingerly as little old ladies. The weather killed business. Then the mercury hovered for weeks around the zero mark, with the air so frigid it hurt to breathe. The black ice cracked over the dried up mud. This arctic cold gripped the entire East Coast, and I wondered how Harry was doing. Was he struggling to please Nancy, bringing her whatever

votive offerings she wasn't allergic to? Were they having
wild sex under the dining room table, thrilled to be together
again? Did they linger over breakfast; take long walks, eat
late suppers at smoky restaurants in the Village? In my imagination they were bathed in a spotlight of domestic bliss,
doing the town like a couple in one of those New York
tourism ads, making love straight out of the Kama Sutra.
Jealousy gnawed at my bones, a persistent little rat I refused
to kick away.

But still I kept going on those arid little dates and struggling with the shop and writing lists of self-improvement
schemes that came to nothing. One February day I hit bottom,
to borrow a phrase from the people in the AA group my
mother had once attended for a week. I'd gone out to Anne
Arundel county in the shuddering Dodge, only to find a basement full of hideous seventies relics – polyester leisure suits,
Quiana shirts, Dacron bodysuits. The heater was on the fritz
all the way home. By the time I had reached my front door
my hands were so numb I could barely open the locks, and my
head was hurting with the keen headache intense cold brings
on. I couldn't get warm all through, even after a scalding bath
and with six blankets over me.

The radiator banged and banged, a knocking sound so loud
it seemed some clanging giant was at the door. I lay in bed
and played the alphabet game. The subject was political figures. I got all the way to Zinoviev before the thought hit me: I
could be alone forever. Everyone else I know would find
someone and I would end up unpaired, solitary, bereft. This
thought occurred to me as one might realize that a symptom
long ignored could be signaling a fatal disease. I, Diana
Campanella, could die alone tonight and no one would find
me until the neighbors were alerted by the smell.

I thought of a night when Harry had told me that I was a
wonderful lover. He had said, 'No one makes love like you

do. It's not like anything I've ever experienced.' At the time
he had seemed to believe it, and I'd felt as if someone had
handed me dozens of red roses. I could have sworn I was with
a man who loved me.

I started to cry. I cried for a long time, sobbing from my
stomach the way a child does. Afterwards I got up and made
a cup of tea. When I glanced out the window I saw it had been
snowing for a while. Several inches were already on the
ground. How beautiful the snow was. I had loved it always.
And I would still love it when I was an old lady, whether
someone was beside me watching it or not. My mother had
not lived to be an old lady. But then she would have hated
being old. She would have seen it as a constant giving up of
all the things that made life as a woman worth living: your
looks, the way men looked at you, the vigilant control you
exercised over your body. But I thought I would like being
old, having been born old.

You always ask yourself if you should give in to the impulse
to write to ex-lovers – whom Cynthia calls 'the unfaithful
departed' after that phrase in the Mass where we remember
those who have gone to their reward. There is so much you
wish you could say to people who are gone, and it's not even
the important stuff, not always. If my mother could come
back, I wouldn't necessarily talk about the shop the first thing.
I'd be more likely to ask her what she thought of my haircut,
or tell her a joke I'd saved for her, waiting all this time just to
watch her crack up. And I think that the same impulse that drives people to seances and Ouija boards – that frantic urge for
the dear old pleasure of talking – operates in failed love
affairs too. What I missed was the luxury of silliness and
smallness Harry and I had shared. You can't write a letter to
your once-lover and point out that the diner you two liked so

much has changed its menu, or that you were walking down
Connecticut Ave. and saw a woolen pullover on sale in the
shade of blue that just matches his eyes. Letters to old lovers
are like telegrams: there is only room to say the important
things, and even then you feel the cruel need for brevity, the
loss of the other person's guaranteed indulgence for your
utterances.

So when I wrote to Harry at last, I came to the point. One
day in March you could smell earth instead of cold in the air,
and the back of winter was broken. That evening I wrote to
him. I wrote to his office address because I didn't know his
home address, and I scrawled 'personal' all over it, but actually I didn't care who read it. All I cared was that it got to him.
I ran the letter down to the mailbox before I could change my
mind. Here is what I wrote:

Dear Harry,

I miss you so much. I know I should have more pride than
this, but I just don't. I don't want to say to myself in ten
years, well, I could have won him back if I'd been a little
less dignified.

You stupid idiot. How often do you expect love like we
had to come along in your life? Most people, you have to
do so much work, just to talk to them. With so many
people, everything is in translation. But with us it's not like
that at all. You said that you told me more than you'd ever
told anyone.

I guess you think that you can work on talking to Nancy.
Work on making her love you. But you can't earn your way
into making her grin like a fool when you come home at
night. You can't earn your way into delighting her the way
you used to delight me. That's something that's given to two
people, like grace.

I go out on dates. I'm even sort of popular again. But I don't get along with anyone the way I got along with you.

I want you back. If it were about rights, I'd say I have as much right to you as Nancy, because there isn't much tenderness in Nancy for you and I'm happy just watching you laugh over some stupid comic strip. But it's not about rights. Remember what you said about religion that day we were walking by the cathedral? That religion was all about where you feel at home? I felt at home with you from our first night together.

I know you won't answer this, but I just wanted to say it while I still had the guts: I love you.

Diana

Chapter XVIII

The writers began laying the groundwork for Brice's disappearance – for Brice had to be out of commission if Simon was going to have his honeymoon. So Brice was making plans to go on a fishing trip in the wilderness of upstate New York. As he planned his trip, Brice daydreamed of Margo Moore, the plucky young occupational therapist whom Brice had been in love with for months, although he didn't know it yet. He simply mused on Margo's kindness to a young girl traumatized in a skiing accident (who would turn out to be the niece of April Dunning and the stepsister of April's psychotic ex-husband Donovan). Brice had a dream one night in which he was kissing Margo, which was thrown in to keep the audience from getting too restless with the creeping pace of the Brice/Margo storyline.

Meanwhile, Charmaine was carrying out her plan to arrange Brice's demise in a canoeing accident. Then she could take over Covington Industries. Charmaine was shown looking at herself in the mirror of her imposing bedroom at Covington Manor and saying, 'When I'm in charge, things will change.'

Margo, though, had not been idle. Working at the hospital as she did, she had already figured out that Charmaine talked Dr. Salter into giving her a prescription for sleeping pills, the same brand that had killed Mrs. Moultrie. The Friday of

Cynthia's shower, the show closed with Margo holding the empty prescription bottle, which she had found hidden under a seat cushion in the old caretaker's gatehouse on the Covington estate.

It was an unconventional shower. Cynthia had insisted, over Francesca's protests, on inviting Paul and his lover Richard. The only other guests were Annette, Rafaella, Francesca and me. Francesca had reserved a back room at The Happy Farmer, a pretentious French restaurant in Alexandria where all the tables were draped in Laura Ashley florals. I knew Cynthia would have preferred to eat Thai food at One Night in Bangkok down on 15th Street. But Francesca had always thought that The Happy Farmer would be perfect for a shower, so that's where we went.

The air that night was balmy as full spring. It was an edgy group. Francesca wouldn't look directly at Paul and Richard. Rafaella was rushed, since this was one of her busiest times of year. We ordered swordfish or lamb from a prix fixe menu.

Paul and Richard gave Cynthia a food processor. Cynthia's psychic Surnami had told her about a diet of pureed grass and strawberries, and she wanted to try it although she didn't need to lose weight.

'Fasting purifies the system,' Cynthia told me. 'Surnami goes on a fast every three months.'

Rafaella's present was a hat to match Cynthia's going-away suit, which was a pale delphinium blue with a fitted jacket. The hat was braided straw with a deep blue velvet ribbon and a dotted veil. Annette brought pewter windchimes for the upper windows of Simon's brownstone, where Cynthia was already living.

My contribution was a moss-green mohair blanket I'd seen Cynthia admire in a shop window in Georgetown. Francesca's was a set of ceramic mixing bowls and the beginner's version of the *Better Homes and Gardens* cookbook, complete with pictures so that you could see what the food should look like at every step.

'Oh wonderful,' said Cynthia, and Francesca's face lit up. The truth was, Cynthia approached the stove only at Christmas and Easter, to make her famous chocolate walnut brownies, and I doubted marriage would change that. Cynthia's cooking was like that scene in *Woman of the Year* where Katherine Hepburn makes a wreck of the kitchen.

'Are you doing okay?' Cynthia asked me while Francesca was showing the others photos of how to make an orange souffle.

'Yeah, I am. I really am.'

'Don't forget all about Harry.'

'I'm sure trying to.'

'I'm not saying sit around hoping, I'm just saying don't forget him.'

'Fine, I'll send a contribution in his name to the Men Are Scum Society.'

'How about I ask him to the wedding after all?'

'No thanks. Did I mention that we broke three thousand last Saturday?'

Normally she would have called me on the abrupt change of subject, but she let it slide.

I told her how suddenly Cynthia's was busy every weekend, and did a fine weekday traffic too. Consignments were coming in so fast that I had to make a rule I wouldn't take them on Saturdays. On my Wednesdays I traveled farther than ever, to the Eastern Shore and west towards Cumberland. Just like my grandfather with his knife-sharpening truck, I had found a business that caused me to trundle around to strangers' homes.

'No more worrying about going back to the Agency,' said Cynthia.

'My old gang there sent chrysanthemums to congratulate

us on the *Dispatch* piece. Some of the women are even regulars.'

'Will wonders never cease,' said Cynthia. 'Did you do
what I told you about the coffee discounts?'

Cynthia thought I should press the coffee bar across the
street for discounts for me and my customers. She thought it
would be a great gimmick. I thought it would be cheesy of
me.

'Let me do it my own way,' I said.

'Yeah, you were doing just great with your own way before
I showed up.'

'Cynthia, I've said thank you a million times. I admit I owe
it all to you. Now can you stop second-guessing me?'

She sniffed a huffy little sniff that made her look exactly
like my mother used to when my mother was referring to girls
who chewed gum or did other unladylike things she wanted
her daughters to avoid. Funny how I had always assumed I was
just like my mother. Cynthia was just like her too, in a different way. After all, Cynthia had reinvented herself in a more
glamorous image, just like my mother. Cynthia had exacting
standards for people, just like my mother. And Cynthia
expected me to play by her rules – just like my mother.

'You look like such a priss when you do that,' I said.

As I said it, I realized how angry I was. I was tired of playing second fiddle to my sisters, exhausted from the struggle of
emulating some airbrushed version of Cynthia I carried
around in my head. No, I would never be as dashing, as
poised, as persuasive as she was. On the other hand, would I
switch with my sister, step into her body, exchange lives? Not
anymore.

'Why are you so crabby?' asked Cynthia.

'I'm not crabby. I don't want you to boss me around, that's
all. I can take it from here.'

She opened her mouth to slap me down verbally. We both

knew that was what she was about to do. She was going to dismiss me, the way my family always did. But that didn't mean I had to dismiss myself.

Maybe she saw my jaw grinding. Maybe she saw some new militant light in my eyes. Because instead of lambasting me, she changed course.

'Well, tell me what else is going on then in *your* shop.' She was smiling as she said it, which was almost as good as an apology.

So I told her how it consoled me to think that the standard of dress at the Agency might actually improve because of Cynthia's. Rafaella worked three days a week now. When business was slow we would tell each stories of our love lives, and drink capuccino from that coffee bar Cynthia wanted me to do the deal with – a place I'd once despised. Now the manager was one of our best customers. We'd had an early spring sale, which we announced with postcards to the mailing list of customers we were beginning to assemble. The day all the dressing rooms were full, with one customer waiting, I bought three pots of pink narcissi from the stall in front of the grocery store to celebrate. They bloomed for weeks on my balcony.

Harry had been my cave, my hearth, my homefire burning. If, after all, I had to go through life without him, something was broken in me forever. There was a tarot card in Cynthia's deck of which one meaning was 'permanent scar on mind'. Being without Harry was like that. But you could go on with a permanent scar, I thought to myself when I got home that night. I had found my niche in the world of work, the spot where I belonged without thinking about it. Work gave me deep solid pleasure that depended on no single human being. When I watched women walk out the door with those striped bags, when I did the books and saw Cynthia's was beginning to thrive – then I knew, as Samuel Butler said, that love is only one of the many passions.

Chapter XVIX

One night a week after Cynthia's shower I was in my apartment, listening to my broken heart tape. I had made it several years ago, after a particularly bad parting with a young reporter who was transferred to Johannesburg. The tape featured these songs: 'Catch the Wind', by Donovan; 'Smoke Gets in Your Eyes', by the Platters; 'More than You Know', by Ella Fitzgerald; 'I Fall in Love Too Easily', by Chet Baker; and Patsy Cline's 'I've Got Your Picture, She's Got You.'

I sat on the floor working on new merchandise tags. They would have a hand-inked look (although they'd actually be printed on heavy ivory and peach paper off Francesca's little home computer). They would each be decorated with an ornate border stolen from a clip art book and a quote from a famous writer about clothes. I got this idea from Chinese fortune cookies – people like little sayings that make them feel special. I was debating about including one by Jane Austen:

> 'It would be mortifying to the feelings of many ladies, could they be made to understand how little the heart of man is affected by what is costly or new in their attire ... Woman is fine for her own satisfaction alone. No man will admire her the more, no woman will like her the better for it. Neatness and fashion are enough for the former,

> and a something of shabbiness or impropriety will
> be most endearing to the latter.

This quote appealed to the iconoclast in me, the one who worshipped at the shrine of ornament for ornament's sake. It described the elderly ladies in my neighborhood who would turn out to do their grocery shopping in their best suits. But it might discourage the average shopper.

I put it to one side and began to copy out a few lines by F. Scott Fitzgerald. It was the scene from *Tender is the Night* where Nicole Diver is about to commit adultery with Tommy Barban:

> 'She put on the first ankle-length day dress that she had owned for many years, and crossed herself reverently with Chanel 16. When Tommy drove up at one o'clock she had made her person into the trimmest of gardens. How good to have things like this, to be worshipped again, to pretend to have a mystery!

The old coach clock Philip had given me ticked away in the corner. Overhead the rain drummed down. It was a week of chilly drenching rains, guaranteeing a verdant spring. 'Verdant' was a word I knew from grade school, when every May we crowned with a wreath of flowers the statue of the Virgin Mary that stood on a little hill overlooking the parking lot. There was a line in one of the May crowning hymns that went, 'In gay and verdant bowers/We haste to crown thee now'. This always made the boys snicker. Cynthia had been May queen one year, in a white organza dress with a blue silk sash.

There was a knock on the door. The neighbors downstairs, probably. They were so sensitive to apartment noise they should have moved to the suburbs years ago. Every few months they would come to my door with pained expressions, asking me to walk more lightly or not play rock music after nine p.m. My rudeness to them varied depending on my mood.

But a glance through the peephole showed it wasn't Neville or Susan. It was Philip. I opened the door instinctively. It wasn't as if I could pretend I wasn't home, anyway. Patsy Kline was mourning full volume.

Philip's hair was wet. He hadn't even slicked it back, just pushed it away with one hand so that it stood up around his forehead in boyish cowlicks. His glasses were fogged. He wore a beat-up olive raincoat I'd always loved, a beige pullover, and khakis. His moroccan loafers gleamed.

'I know it's late,' he said.

'No problem. I'm working.'

Legal pad pages with scrawled quotations littered the floor. The paper with the quote describing Julia's cloth of gold dinner dress from *Brideshead Revisited* was an inch from Philip's foot. I bent to pick it up.

'What are these?' he said, but he did not say it critically.

'Just an idea I had.'

He picked up one from Anita Loos: 'Red may catch a gentleman's eye, but nothing holds his attention like pink or blue,' he read.

'That's for this pastel pink angora sweater I just got in. Of course most of them won't be for any specific piece of clothing.' I heard the defensive note in my voice. Why did I still feel I had to defend myself to Philip?

'You're soaked. You want some tea?'

'That would be nice.'

He held his coat in his hand until I went to take it from him. In the old days he'd have just dropped it over a chair. I brought him a towel from the bathroom. He slung it around his neck, then forgot it. He sat in the big red corduroy arm-chair, one he'd always disliked because it had a loose spring. It felt weird to be making conversation with Philip.

'I heard what happened with Harry,' he said. 'I actually called Rafaella to ask how you were.'

'You win a few, you lose a few.'

'I'm not here to gloat.'

'You can gloat if you want to. You've earned it.'

He leaned forward intently.

'No, Diana, I want to apologize. I was pissed as hell that you cheated on me. But I was complaining about you the other day to a friend, how you lied to me and all that, and she said, "Sometimes women cheat for no reason, but sometimes they cheat for a reason". Of course I didn't take that too well, but I got to thinking about it and I realized you had some reasons.'

'No reasons that should have kept me from being honest with you.'

He waved this remark aside.

'The way I took you for granted. Insulted your sister. Made fun of your business. You were just looking for what you didn't get from me.'

'It was a little more complicated than that. I *did* do you wrong. I could have said something instead of suffering in silence.'

'Whatever it was,' he said, 'somehow I can't make you out to be the villainess anymore. As hard as I've tried.'

His hair was a quarter-inch over his collar. Usually he was religious about haircuts.

The kettle began to whistle. When I came back with our cups, he was sitting on the edge of the chair, as if he expected to be asked to go at any minute. I handed him his teacup and he touched my arm.

'Just tell me something,' he said. 'Do you miss me at all? It wasn't all bad, was it?'

I smoothed his hair back from his forehead.

'Not by a long shot,' I said.

He stood up and hugged me, and the moment I should have pulled out of the hug I didn't, because I was so lonely, so comfortless, and because he looked that way too. We kissed. I thought to myself, I know now what it would have taken to hold my own with Philip. How little we know at the time – how much we know afterwards. And all that knowledge doesn't count for anything after the fact.

Then, as we kept kissing, I thought to myself, screw you, Harry. And having kissed Philip, I felt friendlier and kindlier towards him than I had in a long time. We were old friends, after all, and there had been love between us once.

'I forgot the sugar,' I said, and went back into the kitchen. He followed me. We began kissing again. The friendly, kind feelings persisted. But standing kissing Philip where Harry had kissed me at the sink, I didn't feel only friendly towards Philip. I felt like something urgent and angry and without thought.

'We've never done it standing up,' I whispered.

For a minute he looked taken aback, and then he grinned and went at me, pulling my t-shirt off my shoulder, grabbing me around the waist with one hand while he slid my skirt up with the other. I wanted to undress him too but he had no patience for that. He rushed out of the necessary clothes while I leaned against the wall, watching this new Philip, the one without a strategy, the one who still wanted me. I still wanted him, too, though it wasn't like with Harry.

Philip came back to me. He put the step stool I used to reach the high shelves against the wall. 'Stand on that,' he said. Then he said, 'If you don't mind.' His smile was the sweetest smile he had ever given me.

The step gave an angle of entry, and it made us almost eye

level. It was hot, being pressed against the wall with him driving into me. The step banged against the wall and I was stroking him while he moaned and moaned, until he finally pulled my hand away and held both my hands at my side.

'I don't want to lose it. Not yet,' he said. His beautiful blue-green eyes were misted over with passion, and his thrusting grew less blind, less reflexive as we looked at each other. He slowed it down, then slowed it down some more, and we were more attuned to each other than we had ever been, slow and fluid and graceful as if we were making love under water. He said my name over and over as he came.

He carried me to the couch and we lay there, exhausted. Then he leaned on one elbow and said, 'It isn't gone. It can't be. Not after that.'

So he stayed the night. With Philip lying beside me, with the breathing of another human being in the darkness, I was able to sleep straight through to day for the first time since I'd met Harry that hot June night at my father's. It made me feel I had someone of my own, that I could stand missing Harry if I had to.

In the morning, Philip said, 'This felt like old times again. Better than old times.' After breakfast (bagels and hazelnut coffee he'd run out for), he asked if he could see me again. I didn't say no.

Chapter XX

The morning of Cynthia's wedding was rainy, which was supposed to be good luck. Cynthia, however, took it as a personal insult. She paced her bedroom at the Graham and every five minutes she'd go to the window and yell out at the weather to clear up. This being New York, no one even blinked an eye at a gorgeous woman in an Elizabeth Taylor black silk slip leaning out the window shouting at the sky. And the weather obeyed. By eleven the sun was shining in a tentative way and by twelve-thirty, when we departed for the church, only a few feathery cloud-streaks were left in the baby-blue sky.

Everything had worked out perfectly, even Simon's release from the show. Brice had taken a bullet that Charmaine intended for Margo Moore. After Brice was shot, his kayak overturned, while Margo and Charmaine were swept further down the raging river. Last seen, Brice was unconscious and headed for the falls. He would eventually revive, nursed to health by a kindly couple who owned the country store up the road. They would find him where he had managed to crawl out of the river just before he was carried to his death.

Margo, meanwhile, had bashed Charmaine over the head, but Charmaine was recuperating so nicely in the prison hospital that it was certain she'd be back to cause further trouble. Charmaine's future on the show was far more assured than

Margo's. Plucky young women come and go, but villainesses last forever.

The church was like a golden cave inside, the light from the candles dancing off the Byzantine mosaics. The florist had banked gilt vases of yellow and white roses in front of the altar. Even the air seemed golden. When my sister came down the aisle, I could hear the audible gasp from the guests. She was beautiful beyond the requisite beauty of brides. Simon looked like any nervous groom, not like Brice Covington at all.

It was more like a royal wedding than anything else. The solemnity of the priest, the choreographed movements of Cynthia and Simon as they knelt and stood and exchanged rings, the sermon about the wedding feast of Cana and Christ's smiling on the marriage sacrament, the trumpets playing the recessional procession. Francesca, Annette, and I rode in a rented white Cadillac, behind the bridal limousine, to the Graham. Francesca said, 'Well, that went off very well, don't you think?' 'I said, 'You did a tremendous job. The church looked beautiful. The flowers were a perfect choice.' She sat back and by the happy dreamy look on her face I knew she was ticking off the list of things that would need her supervision at the reception. She had developed an enjoyable ongoing quarrel with the catering director at the Graham.

The Graham is one of those old-fashioned hotels where you expect to see Dorothy Parker arguing at a corner table, or John O'Hara tossing down a whiskey at the bar. The lobby was all burnished wood and faded elegance. There was a fireplace with a fire burning, even though the chill had gone off the day, and a desk backed by rows of bronze mailboxes, as if there were still guests who stayed long enough to receive letters. There had been picture-taking on the church steps and now there was more in the lobby. My eyes were dazzled by the flashbulbs of the guy from *Soap Stories Weekly*.

'Smile,' Francesca hissed in my ear. Her fever of happy efficiency made the color glow in her cheeks. Annette, of course, was beaming and lovely, her own placid self. As for me, I felt like a glamorous imposter in the long filmy dress, the rope of pearls, the Gatsby hat, and the deep red lipstick Cynthia had insisted I wear to match the rose in my hat. For once in my life I felt indubitably pretty. For an instant, I wished Harry could see me. Then I wished he would have a sudden attack of appendicitis and that I would have the good luck to see the ambulance screaming by.

Cynthia felt that head tables had a chilling effect on a party, so the bridesmaids and ushers sat around a table near the swing band, which began to play before dinner was served. Dinner was Cornish game hen and asparagus, and the cake was white chocolate mousse. This would not be one of those weddings where the guests got dry chicken breasts and a few dry broccoli florets.

The lights were dim and seductive – tiny table lamps and the Art Deco sconces on the walls. The walls was decorated with scenes from a naval battle, and the catering director had used potting palms and white wicker loveseats to create all sorts of charming nooks and corners for flirting, gossiping, or passing out. All in all, you felt you had gone back in time to some hopeful moment in the forties just after the war, and that the only thing left to do was get tipsy and dance whenever the swing band played, whether you knew the steps or not.

I sat next to one of Simon's actor friends who amused me with stories of nightmare auditions. Cynthia had her first dance with my father, who was bursting with pride, then a dance with Simon, then with Simon's father. I danced with every usher, with my brother-in-law Jerry, with the best man. A singer in a silver-sequinned evening gown sang war ballads. She sang, 'I'll Be Seeing You', 'We'll Fall Asleep Counting Our Blessings' and 'When Everything You Are Is Mine'.

When she started on 'White Cliffs of Dover', I fled to the ladies room. Sentimental music is the enemy of the lovelorn, like brandy to a recovering alcoholic. After the first wallowing in sorrow, you should avoid it. I hardly played my broken heart tape at all these days.

The stalls at the Graham had thick wooden doors that went down to the ground. I shut myself inside one, adjusted my stockings and removed a piece of lint from the bottom of my shoe. When I emerged, there was Cynthia at the sink, reapplying her lipstick. Next to her was a huge bowl of potpourri which she had shoved aside to make room for her white satin purse, which would be spoiled if water drops got on it. Francesca had forced the hotel to replace all the potpourri in the bathrooms because she thought it didn't smell fresh enough. Cynthia had spilled some. Sprigs of lavender and dried rose petals were scattered over the floor.

'God, you look beautiful,' I said, and removed a stray rose leaf from her dress.

'I have something for you.' She drew a crumpled piece of paper from her bag.

'I saw Harry the day I came up here,' said Cynthia. 'He asked me to give this to you.'

'Why didn't you give it to me before?'

'I thought you should be in the right mood. Not so angry at him. You should have seen him, Diana. He's a wreck.'

The note was on Harry's office stationery.

'Did you read it?' I asked Cynthia.

'Of course.'

I opened the note. It said:

> Hello from your old friend Harry. I know you probably
> won't talk to me, so I'm sending this by Cynthia. I think
> about you often. I wonder what's going on with the shop.
> You may have heard from Cynthia that I moved out again a

few weeks ago. You were right that day at the zoo.

Work is going okay, although they still complain they could use me better in the Washington office.

Remember that day by the river? I know I've been a jerk to you.

If you do feel like talking to me, here is my number. You take care of yourself.

Harry

'What do you think?' said Cynthia.

'What am I supposed to think?'

'Call him, Diana. He needs to be rescued.'

'Why is that my job?'

'Because the poor bastards can never do it themselves. Why don't you go call him now?'

'I'll miss the toasts.'

'To hell with the toasts.'

'He won't be home. It's the middle of a Saturday afternoon.'

'Don't be such a chicken.'

I went out to the lobby in a daze. Another wedding party was arriving. The bride went through the revolving door in a whirl of white tulle. In the background a clerk was saying, 'I'm very sorry madam, but that's hotel policy.'

I chose one of the Graham's polished wood phone booths, slid the door shut and dialed the number. It rang once, twice, three times.

Harry answered.

'Hello Harry.'

'Diana.' His voice sounded, or was it my imagination, full of relief.

'I'm at Cynthia's wedding. She just gave me your note.'

'Just now? I gave it to her days ago.'

'She wanted to wait for the right moment. So how are you?'

'Not so good.'

'How's the wife?'

'Miserable, I'm sure. We don't talk at all these days. It's better that way.'

There was a silence.

'Am I supposed to say I'm sorry, Harry?'

'You know,' said Harry. 'I thought I was doing the right thing coming back here, but it didn't work out the way I thought it would.'

Another silence. I wanted to say, I miss you. I think about you all the time. Philip isn't you. No one is you.

'So how's Philip?' said Harry.

'The same. Look, Harry ...'

'I know you have to go back to things. I know what weddings are like.'

'You walked out on me,' I said. 'You didn't even put up a fight.'

'I'm sorry,' he said.

'That's the best you can do?'

'Be mad at me. I deserve it.'

I said, still angrily, 'I meant what I wrote in my letter.'

'That letter knocked me off my feet.'

'Can you meet me?'

'Right now? You're in the middle of a wedding.'

'To hell with the wedding.'

'You're at the Graham, right? That's what Cynthia told me.'

'You can't come here. There's people, it's ... We'd never make it out the door.'

'What are your cross streets?'

I told him.

'That's near the Columbus Avenue flea market. You'll love the Columbus Avenue flea market. No, you're all dressed up.'

'I don't care about that.'

'I can meet you there in twenty minutes,' Harry said.

'Twenty minutes. Hurry.'

'I love you,' he said, and hung up before I could answer.

I had my purse in my hand. All I had to do was walk out the door. I didn't trust myself to go back in the ballroom. This was a step I had to take without thinking about it too much, like jumping from a moving train.

I walked across acres of lobby. There was a fleur de lis pattern on the carpet that I saw in my dreams for weeks. I had almost reached the door when my father emerged from the men's room.

'What's going on? Where are you going?'

'I have an appointment, Dad.'

'An appointment? An appointment *now*?'

The vein in his forehead was throbbing.

'We're in the middle of your sister's wedding here.'

He was blocking my way to the door. His big heavy body seemed as wide as the Lincoln Tunnel.

'I have to go, Dad. Cynthia knows why.'

'Have you lost your mind? You get back in that ballroom right now.'

His face was thunderous, choked with blood.

'Will you let me get past, Dad.'

He grabbed my arm. I seized his wrist and pulled his hand off.

'Don't ever touch me like that again,' I said.

He looked as shocked as if his dog had bit him. It had taken all my courage to push his hand away, but now suddenly I realized, I was free. He couldn't hurt me anymore. He was just a sorry old man who was marrying off his daughter and wanted everything to be perfect in the old Italian way. But although he loved Cynthia and approved of Annette and Francesca, he would never approve of me. Maybe somewhere deep in his crotchety, judgmental heart he loved me. I was willing to consider the possibility, but not right now. Right now I had to get to Harry.

So I walked around my father and left him standing there. On the sidewalk all was chaos. Bellboys hustled luggage. A woman in a fur coat directed them. I turned to a doorman.

'How do I get to the Columbus Avenue flea market?'

He didn't even blink.

'You go up two blocks. Turn right on —. Left on —. You can't miss it.'

The Columbus Avenue flea market was set up on the blacktop of an elementary school. In the bright April air there were tables and tables of merchants. Dimestore mittens crowded nesting Russian dolls. Plaster angels hung from a clothesline. Against the chainlink fence someone had pinned lace camisoles, crocheted baby dresses, men's smoking jackets and velvet turbans. One folding table was piled with crystal sugar dishes and ashtrays, factory seconds. In the corner where the lingering sun shown strongest, a man sold only suspenders. I wanted to buy Harry a pair, and then it occurred to me that I'd never seen him in suspenders. And then I thought, well, why not, and for five dollars bought an enamel blue pair with a faint silver stripe. At every table there were people asking questions, handling someone's grandmother's cameo and someone's cousin's paper lampshades, someone's aunt's old stole with a dangling fox head, someone's clay honey pot.

There was a smell of roast chestnuts, a smell I always associated with New York. Next to me a man and woman were debating where to go for dinner. It sounded like a pleasurable debate. The Italian place on 49th? Thai? Not Mexican, they had had Mexican the other night. He held their baby, a chubby baby with rosy cheeks in a pink crochet cap.

The world was so much bigger than my family. Nobody

knew who I was; I was anybody. For the first time in my life I felt happy to be in a crowd, part of the bazaar. I was no different from any merchant here – you have your little table or your little rooms, you try to sell what you love in the hope someone else will love it too. We do it all our lives.

The light was turning blue and rose and people were beginning to leave in chattering clumps. I could feel Harry getting nearer, feel him hurrying down these narrow streets to me.

Then he was there. I waited for him to come to me. He walked across the blacktop and grabbed me up and held me so hard my ribs hurt. Then he put me down and said, 'I can't believe you're here. I can't believe it.'

'This doesn't mean you're home free,' I said to Harry. 'I don't want you to think I'm a pushover.'

'I'd never call you a pushover,' said Harry, but he was grinning.

All the delicate negotiations and trials of love were ahead of us, if we were among the lucky ones who lasted more than a month or a day. But here he was. He hadn't thought twice about it. So I wasn't afraid – or not as afraid as I used to be.

'Let's go to a bar,' I said to Harry. 'I want to sit in a corner and hear the story of your life.'

'I thought we already did that,' said Harry, smiling.

'We're just getting started,' I said. 'Tell me about one of your miserable childhood experiences, and I'll tell you about one of mine.'

He slung his arm around my shoulder.

'Did I ever mention the time Sheldon took me to see the Intrepid?'

Chapter XXI

Three months later, Harry moved back down to Washington and in with me. His firm was pleased to send him, and their business has picked up enough to keep him here indefinitely. His divorce from Nancy was final six months ago. I celebrated the occasion with an indecently alluring red teddy – and by keeping my mouth shut about what a blessed deliverance losing Nancy was. To give Harry credit, he knows it. He even shakes his head in bewilderment about his marriage once in a while, a sure sign of recovery.

As for Cynthia's, it's doing so well now that I had to lease the space downstairs when the owner of the shoe repair shop retired. Now I have a full-time assistant, and Rafaella still works part-time. The profit margin is small, and running a shop will never be as easy as marking time at the Agency was, but then I guess I must be happier when things don't come easy.

Cynthia and Simon are planning their first child. Cynthia counts on conceiving in September, so that she won't have to be pregnant during any summer months. I'm sure it will go according to plan, right down to a three-hour labor and a three-week return to a size six.

Cynthia has opened a shop of her own in the Village. It's called Cornerstone, and it sells all sorts of ornamental building artifacts, from glass doorknobs to stone entrance urns, from marble mantelpieces to antique mirrors. She's already on a first-name basis with half the interior decorators and contractors in town – 'All the important ones, anyway,' she says. Eventually she wants a national clientele and a glossy catalog. If anyone knows catalogs, it's Cynthia. When she has that baby, who knows, *RosePetal*'s may even consider a maternity line.

Simon has cheered up a lot since they married. His prep school accent has become fainter and fainter. Last time they visited he even shot hoops with Harry and my brothers over at Infant Martyrs' new gym. 'Brand new Filas,' Harry said shaking his head, but I could see he gave Simon credit for the effort.

Philip took my return to Harry gracefully if more sadly than I'd have thought. Lately he's been dating a woman whom he met at his riding stables in Middleburg. Harry and I ran into them outside the coffee bar the other day. Her name is Tricia. She has blonde hair in a simple pageboy, a few freckles, and a degree from Vassar, where her mother went to school with Philip's mother. She wore a plaid kilt and a boiled wool jacket, and after five minutes she said, 'We'd better go, honey. We have to pick up Cleo at the kennel.' Cleo, it turned out, is their Irish setter, so it seems to have gotten pretty serious. Philip looked content and well-cared-for, as he'd never looked with me. Which just goes to show, I said to Harry, that you should never try to divert someone from his natural course.

Francesca and my father are speaking to me again, although it took a few months after Cynthia's wedding for that. When Francesca asks when Harry and I are getting married, I say airily, 'We've talked about it. We may never bother, and then again we could run off to Reno tomorrow.' Francesca sighs, but even she can see I mean it, that I don't really care if or when, although Harry mentions it more often now that his divorce is final. I used to think of marriage as a golden crown, as proof of my worthiness to be loved. Now I think of it as maybe a nice idea, but then again why tempt fate? I will never be so at ease in the universe that I wouldn't prefer God not to catch me being happy.

Besides, Francesca has other potential marriages than mine to worry about. My father now takes Mrs. Giampetroni to the Old Stein for the bratwurst and beer special every Thursday night. Bratwurst is her favorite, since she started life as Hilda Metzbaum. On Friday nights they go dancing at the Spanish Ballroom, and once a month they host the Saturday poker game. We all interpret this as a sign that wedding bells may ring out again in our family sometime soon. For Francesca's sake I hope so. She needs another family event to plan, another catering director to torture.

I still worry. I always will. I still believe that Harry is mine on loan, that my shop could fold tomorrow, that nothing I have earned will last forever. When Harry comes home at night and stays the night and then comes home the next night, it still surprises me. When he tells a joke I still laugh even if I've heard it before. We're alike that way. He still wakes up if I leave the bed at night. He still expects the sky to fall or his mother, at least, to contract a lingering illness as punishment for his daring to love a woman instead of simply enduring one. We are still skittish about saying 'we' and 'our' like other couples do. Together, we take very little for granted.

One hot summer night, a night very like the night we met, Harry turned to me and said, 'Do you think we'll ever relax? Do you think we'll ever plan on being happy? Maybe start a retirement account?'

'I don't know,' I said. In the corner the air conditioner groaned and appeared to stop dead. Harry got up and banged its side. It sputtered into life again. It might not last another summer or he could still be doing that in ten years. Who knew?

'Do you mind?' I said to Harry.

'Mind what?' said Harry.

'That I'll never learn to cook properly. That we'll never own the right furniture. That our relatives will always disapprove.'

'Do I mind that you always put five extra dollars of postage on every package because you're afraid the mailman won't deliver it without an extra bribe? Do I mind that you always have to sit at the end of the row at the movies in case there's a fire? Not if you don't mind that I'll never make partner or buy you a vacation home at the Eastern Shore. By the way, I'll stand in line for you at the post office next time.'

'I'd never make you stand in line.'

Harry kicked his shoes in a corner and threw his shirt over a chair. Then he climbed into bed and kissed me, a real kiss, not just a token goodnight kiss like I used to get from Philip and he used to get from Nancy.

'There are worse ways to live,' Harry said.